Praise for

Campus Cravings

This fast-paced story started with a bang and never let up until the very end...This inspiring story shows the difference one person can make to the lives of others if they just take the time to get involved.
~ *Fallen Angel Reviews*

It's another entertaining read set in the college world inhabited by the characters of Campus Cravings, but this time the subject matter is far more serious than usual...The pacing is smooth, the personalities are well-developed and the sex sizzling hot...
~ *Literary Nymphs Reviews*

Total-E-Bound Publishing books by Carol Lynne:

Campus Cravings Volume One: On the Field
Coach
Side-Lined

Sacking the Quarterback

Campus Cravings Volume Two: Off the Field
Off Season
Forbidden Freshman

Campus Cravings Volume Three: Back on Campus
Broken Pottery
In Bear's Bed

Campus Cravings Volume Four: Dorm Life
Office Advances
A Biker's Vow

Campus Cravings Volume Five: BK House
Hershie's Kiss
Theron's Return

Campus Cravings Volume Six
Incoming Freshman
A Lesson Learned

Good-Time Boys
Sonny's Salvation
Garron's Gift
Rawley's Redemption
Twin Temptations

Cattle Valley Volume One
All Play & No Work
Cattle Valley Mistletoe

Cattle Valley Volume Two
Sweet Topping
Rough Ride

Brookside Athletic Club
I'll Stand By You

Neo's Realm Volume One
Liquid Crimson
Blood Trinity

Healing Doctor Ryan
Moor Love
Highland Gaymes
Stolen Memories
Corporate Passion
Dalton's Awakening
Reunion
Sunset Ridge
Broken Colour

CAMPUS CRAVINGS
Volume Seven

Locky in Love

The Injustice of Being

CAROL LYNNE

Campus Cravings Volume Seven
ISBN # 978-1-78184-552-4
©Copyright Carol Lynne 2012
Cover Art by PoshGosh ©Copyright 2012
Interior text design by Claire Siemaszkiewicz
Total-E-Bound Publishing

Published in 2012 by Total-E-Bound Publishing, Think Tank, Ruston Way, Lincoln, LN6 7FL, United Kingdom.

LOCKY IN LOVE

Chapter One

"BK House," Charlie Salinger answered.

Becket smiled for the first time in a month. "Hey, it's Becket."

"Staying out of trouble?"

"What fun would that be?" Becket rested his feet on the porch railing. "I was wondering, I know I'm not signed up for summer classes, but do you think it would be possible for me to come back early?"

"Why would you want to? The campus is dead this time of year."

"I live in a town of thirteen hundred and thirty-four people stuck out in the middle of fucking corn fields. Believe me, you don't know the first thing about dead." Without a car of his own, Becket was forced to drive the dirt roads of Crescent Ridge, Iowa, in his grandpa's old rusted out pickup. It would be different if his dad actually needed his help on the farm, but with three older brothers, all living and working on the six-hundred and seventy acre spread, Becket's help wasn't needed or wanted.

"Locky's not here if that's what you're hoping for," Charlie informed Becket.

Resident Assistant Lockland Regent was the golden unicorn, the one man Becket continued to drool over but had never been able to conquer. It didn't seem to matter how many times he caught Locky looking at him with lust in his eyes, he always turned Becket away when the offer was made.

"What about Fallon?" The uncle of one of his old housemates may not have been Becket's first choice, but Fallon was hot and rich, two of his favourite things. Besides, for some reason, Fallon's ongoing interest in getting Becket into bed seemed to infuriate Locky.

"Stay away from Fallon. He's too damn old for you," Charlie scolded.

Becket grinned. Forbidden fruit always tasted better. "Will you let me come? I'll pay."

"You'll clean. This place needs a good cleaning from top to bottom before the fall semester, and since I obviously can't do it, and Jack's taken a job at one of the local diners for the summer, we were planning to hire it out. However, since you have the time, you can do it in exchange for room and board. How's that?"

The thought of cleaning the house made Becket groan. He weighed the work involved against his need to be within a two mile radius of gay bars and, as usual, his sex drive won out. "Fine."

* * * *

Locky loosened his tie after a long day and fixed himself a Jack and Coke. The money he earned practicing law at his father's firm would pay his bills for the rest of the year, but the clients he dealt with made him feel dirty at the end of the day.

"Lockland, are you joining us for dinner this evening?" his mother, Gloria Regent, asked.

"Not tonight. I'm meeting friends." Locky took another sip of his drink and settled himself on the tufted red leather sofa in the den. He cursed himself for giving up his apartment, but it didn't make sense to hold onto the damn thing when he was only home three months out of the year.

"Will Brooks be driving you?" Gloria asked.

The last thing Locky needed was for the family chauffeur to know his business. "No, I'll drive myself."

"Well, be careful, dear," Gloria said before leaving the room.

Locky finished his drink before going up the back staircase to his bedroom suite. He had no plans to meet friends, but he did hope to get laid. It wasn't often that he went in search of a random partner for the night, but he needed to get Becket out of his head and his dreams.

Showered and dressed to impress, Locky left the house. He ate a quick dinner at his favourite restaurant in Portland before arriving at the club around ten-thirty. It was still early for the usual crowd, but that suited him fine. He had a few ghosts he needed to exorcise before he'd be in a party mood anyway.

"Hey, Bobo," Locky greeted the owner. He'd known Bobo for years and had even helped him out of a few tickets early in his career. It was the first time he'd stepped foot in the club since the night that had changed his life.

Bobo's blue eyes opened wide. "Locky?" He grabbed Locky into a bear hug, fitting for someone of Bobo's large size. "I didn't think I'd ever see you again."

It had been almost two years since Locky had left Bobo's Bar late one night, slightly tipsy and rejuvenated after a blowjob in the bathroom, to stumble upon a young man beaten and dying beside his car. Despite his best attempts, the guy, Steven Rajos, had died in Locky's arms, forever changing the way he viewed his future. "I figured it was time."

Bobo released him and went around behind the bar. "What can I get ya?"

"Jack and Coke." Locky crossed his arms and rested them on the familiar scarred wood surface. Even after moving away, he still kept track of the local news, hoping the police would catch the group who had beaten Steven, but still nothing. "Any more trouble?"

Bobo handed Locky his drink. "Not like that night, not here anyway. There've been similar incidents at other clubs, but the kids all made it."

"And the cops still don't have any leads." Locky had talked to the detective who handled the case several times since he'd left Oregon and they still couldn't seem to track the fuckers down.

Bobo shrugged. "Hasn't slowed people down. This place is still packed almost every Thursday, Friday and Saturday nights."

The thought of another kid getting hurt simply because they were gay made Locky sick to his stomach.

"Hey, boss, did you order toilet paper?"

Locky turned to see who had spoken and couldn't believe how much the man looked like Becket, same dark curls, same big brown eyes. He leant back against the bar and stared at the younger man with appreciation.

"In the storeroom," Bobo grumbled.

When Locky's cock started to harden, he decided to do something about it. He stood and crossed the room to stand in front of the cute twink. "I'm Locky. I don't think we've met."

The younger man shifted the mop to his left hand before reaching out to accept Locky's offered greeting. "Trent, and I'm new."

"My nineteen-year-old nephew," Bobo added.

Figured. "Nice to meet you." Locky withdrew his hand and shook his head at the loss.

"Get back to work," Bobo ordered.

"It was nice to meet you." Trent licked his bottom lip as his gaze travelled up and down Locky's body.

"You, too." Locky didn't mind the appreciative stare, he was well used to it, but he hated that Trent wasn't old enough to play with. He rejoined Bobo at the bar. "Sorry, I didn't know."

"He's a good boy, but I promised my sister I'd keep him out of trouble." Bobo passed Locky a fresh drink. "And I can tell by the way you were looking at each other, that's exactly what you both had in mind."

"Don't worry about me. I have a strict rule about messing with guys under twenty-one." If he didn't stick to his rule, he'd lose not only his self-respect, but his job as well. His mind wandered to Becket. Shit, physically that guy pressed every one of Locky's buttons. It was only Becket's immature, careless attitude about life and sex that served to remind Locky of his age.

Bobo's growl broke the spell.

"What?" Locky asked, taking a sip of his drink.

"You're daydreaming of someone, and I hope for your sake it isn't my nephew."

"Nah, there's this kid in Idaho that I can't stop thinking about," Locky confessed.

"Let me guess, he's under twenty-one?"

"You got it. Plus, he lives in the house where I work, double no-no."

"How young is this kid?"

"Twenty. He'll be twenty-one around Halloween, but he'll still be living at BK House." Locky ran his fingers through his hair. Since the night of Demitri's Super Bowl party when he'd made the unforgivable mistake of kissing Becket, Locky hadn't been able to get the taste of the younger man out of his system.

Bobo leaned against the bar, putting his face right in front of Locky's. "Take it from me, finding someone to spend your life with is a hell of a lot more important than any job you'll ever have."

"Easy for you to say, you've got Mike and this place."

Bobo's eyes filled with tears. "Mike left me last year, said he was tired of sitting home by himself every night." He stood up. "And like a proud fool, I let him go."

"I'm sorry to hear that. I liked Mike. But you can't really compare what the two of you had to me and Becket. As I said, he's young and immature. Hell, I doubt the kid knows what monogamy is, let alone love."

"Maybe so, just don't count him out because you're afraid of losing your job. Besides, you could have any man you wanted, outside my nephew, of course. The fact that you're hung up on this one guy tells me you like him more than you're willing to admit."

No longer in the mood to hook-up, Locky finished his drink. "It was nice seeing you again, but I think I'll take off."

"Don't be a stranger." Bobo shook his head when Locky withdrew his wallet. "It's on me."

"Thanks." Locky left, feeling worse than he had going in. He bypassed the parking lot and walked to his car down the street from the bar. Although he'd heard what Bobo had to say loud and clear, he still doubted Becket could ever settle down.

* * * *

Sitting on his bed, Becket called Fallon Bennett. It had been a while since he'd spoken to Fallon, but hopefully the hunky older man hadn't forgotten him.

"Hello?"

"Fallon? It's Becket. Do you remember me?"

"Of course I remember you. How're you doing?" Fallon asked.

"Bored. I got back in town last night and thought maybe we could get together." Becket crossed his fingers and hoped Fallon didn't already have plans for the evening.

"I'd love to, but I'm stuck at the club. Feel like stopping by and keeping me company here?"

"Which club?"

"Mine, Fallon's on Fifth. It won't open for another week or so, but you're welcome to come by for a personal preview."

"I'd love to." Becket prayed Fallon already had beer onsite. He loved Charlie and Jack, but they refused to let him drink while living at BK. "I assume it's on Fifth Street, what's the exact address?"

"Just get off the bus at Fifth and Strong, we're at the end of the block, you can't miss it."

"Cool. See you in a few minutes."

"Can't wait."

Becket hung up and checked himself out in the mirror once more. Dressed in skintight jeans and a white, lightweight cotton T-shirt that was practically transparent, he definitely gave off an 'Available and looking for fun' vibe. *Perfect.*

He ran down the stairs, two at a time, before yelling down the hall, "I'm going out."

"Got your key?" Jack asked from inside his and Charlie's apartment.

"Yeah."

"Be safe," Charlie added.

Safe. Becket backtracked to the bathroom and selected two condoms from the provided communal stash. With protection in his pocket, Becket left BK and headed for the bus stop.

It was a short ten-minute ride to the corner of Fifth and Strong and, before he knew it, he was standing in front of Fallon's new place. He stared up at the big expensive-looking sign and shook his head. Fallon's sign was over-the-top, just like the man himself. Becket wouldn't doubt the damn thing cost more than all the other signs on the block combined.

He tried the door but found it locked. He used his fist to pound against the chrome and glass door and waited. Several moments later, the door opened to the view of a scrumptious, shirtless man in work jeans. "Can I help you?"

"I'm Becket, Fallon's expecting me." The small gold hoop running through one of the man's nipples captured Becket's attention. "Nice," he said when he was caught staring.

The man stepped back and let Becket in before locking up again. "If you like that, you'd love the one in my cock."

"Jigger, leave Becket alone," Fallon said, crossing the room.

Becket threw his arms around Fallon and gave him a quick kiss in greeting. "It's good to see you again." He felt Fallon's hands land on his ass and pull him closer.

"I figured that Neanderthal from the party had stolen you for himself." Fallon continued to knead Becket's ass as he kissed his neck.

As much as he wished he could say differently, Becket had finally concluded that, until he was older himself, Locky would be a lost cause. "He doesn't want me. He just doesn't want anyone else to have me."

"His loss." Fallon kissed Becket again, tickling the inside of Becket's mouth with his tongue.

Damn, Fallon was good. Becket was hard within minutes and ready to take things to the next level. "Do you have an office somewhere close?"

"Yes, and unfortunately, it's currently occupied by a man from the Alcohol Beverage Control Bureau. If you can wait around for another half an hour or so, I'll show you my apartment upstairs."

"So no beer?" Becket groaned and ran his hands over Fallon's chest. He unbuttoned Fallon's white dress shirt enough to lick one of Fallon's small nipples. "I was really looking forward to loosening up a bit."

Fallon buried his fingers in Becket's hair and whispered in his ear, "Tell Jigger to get you a glass from my private stash and wait for me upstairs."

Becket groaned when Fallon pulled away. There was nothing in the world like being held by a bigger, stronger man. "Please tell the guy in your office anything he wants to hear so he'll get out of here."

"That *guy* is the key to me opening next week." Fallon slapped Becket's ass on his way by. "Take care of Becket while I'm gone," he told Jigger.

Jigger grinned. "You heard the man."

"Booze, he wants you to give me booze, nothing else."

Jigger stared at Becket for several moments. "He said you could go upstairs?"

"Yeah, ask him if you don't believe me." Becket didn't like the jealous note to Jigger's voice. Was he sleeping with Fallon? "You going to show me upstairs, or should I find my own way?"

"I'll take you, don't get your panties in a wad." Jigger led Becket to a door at the back of the club.

When Jigger gestured for Becket to go first, Becket shook his head. "I'll follow you." There was something about Jigger that made him uncomfortable. Sure the guy was good looking, but he couldn't help feeling that Jigger had something going with Fallon. He waited until he entered the apartment. "Are you sleeping with Fallon?"

"Who isn't?" Jigger laughed, his back to Becket. "Kid, if you're looking for a boyfriend, you've got the wrong guy. Fallon's cool, but he likes 'em young and only a night at a time." He handed Becket a drink.

Becket smelt the mahogany-coloured liquid. *Strong.* He wasn't big on liquor, but he didn't have the guts to tell Jigger that, so he downed the drink in one long gulp. "You're not young, and he's obviously fucking you."

"No one fucks me, boy." Jigger took Becket's empty glass and refilled it. "Sit down and don't touch anything," he warned, before leaving Becket alone in the apartment.

Becket took two sips of the second glass before his vision started to blur. He'd never been a huge drinker, but he wasn't a damn lightweight either. In an effort to gather his wits, Becket shook his head, but the action only made him dizzier.

With his head swimming, Becket had little choice but to stretch out on the sofa. Staring at the swirling ceiling fan was the last he remembered before he passed out.

* * * *

Becket groaned when someone shoved him, trying to rouse him from his deep sleep. "Ten more minutes," he mumbled.

"Not likely, not unless you want the whole street to see you like this," a deep voice replied.

The statement didn't make any sense. Becket rolled over and winced at the hard bed under his sore body. He opened his eyes and stared up at Jack. "What's going on?"

"Thought you said you had your key." Jack took a sip of his coffee and shook his head. "Come on, I'll help you inside."

Inside? Becket lifted his head and looked around. He was on the front porch instead of upstairs in his bed. Birds singing, cars driving by, sprinklers watering, were all indications that another day had begun, but Becket's mind was still on the previous night. "What am I doing out here?"

"Beats the hell out of me. I guess you were too drunk to get yourself inside." Jack set his coffee cup on the porch before helping Becket to his feet.

Becket wobbled as he tried to piece together the events that had landed him in the position he currently found himself in. "I wasn't drunk."

"Sure. You just decided it was a nice night to camp out." Jack picked up his cup before ushering Becket inside. "Go take a shower. You smell like a whore house." He pointed Becket towards the staircase. "I'll make you some breakfast."

Becket used both hands on the banister to help himself climb the steps. *I had one drink,* he told himself. *One and a half, maybe.* With the house virtually empty, he went straight to the bathroom instead of stopping by his room. His first look at himself in the mirror made everything worse. "Shit."

Becket ran a hand over the hickeys on his neck. Wondering how far down they went, he pulled his filthy shirt off over his head. His entire chest and torso were covered in small bruises, like someone had made a meal of him. "What the fuck?"

He reached into his jeans pocket and came out with two unwrapped condoms. Playing it safe had always been a hard and fast rule with him. Becket crossed to the row of showers and turned one on, praying whoever he'd been with had supplied their own protection.

Fallon. He suddenly remembered falling asleep on Fallon's couch. With his hands on his zipper, he remembered Fallon trying to wake him up. Bits and pieces of the previous night began to come back to him. Fallon talking to Jigger as Becket tried to keep his eyes open.

Becket toed out of his sneakers and pushed his jeans down. Somewhere along the way he'd lost his underwear. The thought of someone finding them mortified him, but not as much as the dried streaks of cum running down the inside of his thigh. "Fuck. Fuck. Fuck!" he yelled, the sound bouncing off the tiled walls.

He jumped under the spray and grabbed for the soap, hoping to erase the evidence of his careless night. After scrubbing himself from head to toe, Becket didn't feel any cleaner. Although he still didn't know who he'd had sex with, one thing became perfectly clear, he'd been drugged and fucked without protection.

Becket took his anger out on the wall, punching his fist against the tile. The sickening crunch of bone quickly gave him something else to focus on. He didn't hold back his scream. The pain of his injured hand helped cover the anguish over his broken spirit. As he sank to the floor, Becket knew he'd never look at his world the same way.

Chapter Two

Becket stared at the royal blue cast that had decorated his forearm to his second knuckle for the last two weeks. He'd lied to the doctor, Charlie and Jack about what had prompted his self-inflicted injury. What had happened during the hours he couldn't account for was no one's business but his own. He'd gone to Fallon's with one goal in mind, and although he knew in his gut he'd been drugged, he obviously got fucked. Mission accomplished, right?

"Yo," Chase greeted, flopping onto the couch beside Becket. "Charlie told me what happened. That blows, man."

"Yeah." Becket returned his attention to the television. Chase was a good guy who'd come back to campus early to settle in before football practice started, but Becket wasn't in the mood to talk.

Chase put his feet up on the coffee table and crossed his arms over his chest. "Something else going on?"

Becket ignored the question. Charlie had evidently sent Chase in on a fact-finding mission. He tossed the remote in Chase's lap. "Watch what you want." He left the room before he could be questioned further. "Nice try," he told Charlie as he passed through the living room.

"He's just worried," Jack replied, sticking up for his partner.

"Yeah, well, I appreciate it, but like I told you, there's nothing wrong." Becket left the house and stood on the front porch in the same spot where someone, probably Fallon, had dumped him a couple of weeks earlier.

Becket moved to sit on the step. He'd considered going down to Fallon's place and confronting him about the missing hours, but what was the point? It was over, and he had no proof, not even memories of what had happened.

"The athletes will start trickling in within the next week or so," Jack said from behind Becket.

"Is that your subtle way of telling me to get back to work?" Becket glanced over his shoulder. Jack was a conundrum. He looked mean, like someone you'd never want to approach, but he was so caring with Charlie, and when the situation called for it, with the other guys in the house.

Jack moved to sit beside Becket. "Well, you do need to finish painting the bathroom, or do you have something against Egyptian Gold?"

Becket rolled his eyes. The paint colour sucked, but Charlie had convinced Jack that yellow would revive young college students after a late night of studying. Jack, being the supportive, but decoratively challenged retired Marine that he was, had picked up gold paint without taking into account how the hue would look on the wall or the fact that yellow did not necessarily translate to gold. "It's a little much, and when I brush my teeth in the morning, I don't like the green version of me staring back in the mirror."

"You're full of shit. That gold is rich-looking."

Becket chuckled. It was obvious Jack was proud of the paint he'd chosen. "You're right, it is rich-looking, but I think it would work better in the kitchen. Why don't I pick up something more…sunny, for the bathroom?"

Jack rubbed the back of his neck. "Promise me you won't tell Charlie that I fucked up the colour thing?"

Becket bumped his shoulder against Jack. He'd been so involved in the conversation that for the first time in weeks, he'd been able to put his own problems aside. "It'll be our secret. Just let me do the choosing from now on."

"Fine." Jack thumped Becket on the back before standing. "I'm taking Charlie to Fallon's grand opening tonight. Interested in tagging along?"

Becket swallowed around the lump of fear lodged in his throat. "No."

"You sure? Dane'll be there."

"Drop it." Becket's temporary good mood slid back into the gutter. He got to his feet and regarded Jack, ready to defend his decision further, but shook his head, realising it wasn't worth it. "Later."

* * * *

With a suitcase in each hand and one tucked under his arm, Locky let himself into BK House. He set his bags down and took a deep breath. The house smelt like fried chicken, something that was never allowed in his parents' house. And just like that, Locky was freed of the opulent and oppressive life he'd grown up with.

"Hey," Chase greeted, running down the staircase. "Dinner's ready."

"Coming." Locky left his suitcases where they were and followed Chase into the dining room. "Just in time," he announced, pulling out a chair.

"Have you washed your hands?" Charlie asked.

Locky paused in the act of sitting down. "Be right back." He left the table and entered the kitchen, stopping short when he almost ran into Becket. "Excuse me."

Head down, Becket nodded and kept going. The flash of blue on Becket's forearm caught Locky's attention, but by the time he opened his mouth to ask, the younger man was already out of the room.

Locky quickly washed his hands and returned to the dining room. He was surprised that Becket wasn't at the table with Charlie, Jack and Chase. "Where'd Becket go, and what the hell did he do to his arm?"

The three men at the table suddenly looked uncomfortable, but it was Charlie who finally spoke up. "He's eating in his room, just like he's done every night since he broke his hand."

"How'd that happen?" Locky sat in his usual spot and reached for the platter of chicken. It bothered him that no one had called to tell him about the accident.

Charlie cleared his throat and pointed his fork towards Chase. "We'll talk about it after dinner."

Chase snorted. "Hey, if you want me to get lost, just tell me."

"Get lost," Jack said without missing a beat. "*After* you eat your dinner."

Chase returned his attention to the mound of mashed potatoes and homemade fried chicken gravy. "Don't have to tell me twice," he mumbled around a mouthful of food.

Locky filled his plate, but found he wasn't as hungry as he'd first thought. "Why's Becket here anyway? Classes don't start for another three weeks."

"I think Iowa bored him, so he called and asked if he could come early. I've put him to work getting the rooms ready," Charlie explained.

"Well he can't do much with one hand." Locky had a good idea why Iowa bored Becket, hell, he was bored just thinking about it.

"He does well enough," Jack said in Becket's defence.

Locky glanced at Jack. Usually, Jack was hard on the residents, but it sounded like Becket had managed to slip under Jack's skin. He wondered if Jack's protective streak had something to do with the reason Becket had broken his hand. He decided to concentrate on his dinner and wait for answers. By the way Chase was shovelling his food in, it wouldn't be long.

Five minutes later, Chase sat back and rubbed his flat stomach. "I'm stuffed."

"Glad you liked it. Now get lost." Jack reached for another biscuit and the bottle of honey.

"I'm *supposed* to do the dishes tonight. *However*, I'd be able to hear your entire conversation from the kitchen. Are you sure you want me in there eavesdropping?" Chase took his time picking up his plate, no doubt hoping for a reprieve.

"Go upstairs and get those headphones you always have stuck in your ears. You can listen to some of that rap crap you kids listen to while you work," Jack ordered, refusing to let Chase slack off on his chore.

Chase groaned and rolled his eyes, reminding Locky of how young he was. Chase may have the body of a man, but he definitely acted like a nineteen-year-old.

Jack chuckled after Chase stomped out of the room. "I can't blame him for trying. That cast iron skillet's gonna be a bitch to clean."

"So tell me, what's going on with Becket?" Locky gave up the pretence of eating and pushed his plate towards the centre of the table.

"The night after he arrived, he went out. I found him the following morning asleep on the porch. I figured he'd gotten plastered and knew better than to come into the house in that condition, but I think there's more to it," Jack explained.

"He broke his hand and he won't tell you how he did it?" Locky was confused.

"No, he broke his hand in the shower. I told him to get cleaned up and the next thing I knew, he came downstairs, soaking wet, cradling his hand." Jack shook his head. "Since then, he's been a completely different guy, and he won't let anyone in, but he leaves every night dressed like a slut and gets home in the middle of the night."

"He's always dressed like that." Going out every single night sounded excessive, even for Becket, but Locky could rationalise it if Becket had been cooped up in his small hometown for most of the summer.

"No, not like this." Jack sighed. "It isn't just the clothes or the going out either. Becket rarely talks to us anymore, and he just looks so…sad all the time."

The man Jack described sounded nothing like the flirt he'd run away from only two months earlier. One of Becket's biggest faults was telling people too much information about his social life, so for him to suddenly shut down started a nagging feeling in Locky's gut. "I wonder if he'd talk to me?"

"I doubt it, but it can't hurt to try." Charlie stood and started out of the room. "I think Chase must've gotten lost."

After Charlie left, Jack leaned on the table, putting himself closer to Locky. "I don't think I've ever seen Charlie this worried. He hasn't slept a full night since it happened, so anything you could do to ease his mind would be appreciated."

Locky got to his feet. "I'll take care of my suitcases then go up and see if he'll talk to me."

* * * *

After stowing his luggage in his small apartment on the third floor, Locky walked down a flight of stairs to Becket's room. He knocked twice before the door opened. "Hey."

"Can I help you?" Becket was naked from the waist up, showing off his leanly muscled chest.

Locky zeroed in on Becket's dark brown nipples before he mentally slapped himself and turned his gaze to the blue cast decorating his right hand. "That's gonna make it hard to write once classes start."

Becket shrugged. "It'll probably be off by then, but if it's not, I'll make it work." He moved to his closet and pulled out a long-sleeved shirt. "Anything else?"

Staring at Becket, Locky couldn't reconcile the man who stood in front of him with the chatty, happy-go-lucky kid he'd last seen a few months earlier. Taking in the long-sleeved shirt and dead stare of Becket's big brown eyes, stomach acid began to do a number on Locky's digestion. "What happened to you that night before Jack found you asleep on the porch?"

Becket took a step back. "What I did or didn't do is none of your goddamn business. Now if you'll excuse me, I have somewhere to be."

Becket tried to step past Locky, but Locky moved in front of him, blocking his path. "If someone hurt you, you can tell me."

With more force than Locky would expect, Becket slammed his casted arm across Locky's chest. "Why would I tell you anything? I poured my fucking heart out to you and you had the nerve to tell me I was too young to know what I was talking about." He gave Locky's chest another shove and moved past him into the hallway. "If you hadn't been such a dick none of this would've happened."

"What happened? Tell me!" The tone of Locky's voice was harsher than he'd intended, but Becket was beginning to really worry him.

"Just leave me alone." Becket started towards the stairs. "You're good at that," he said before descending.

Locky rested his hands on his hips, unsure of his next move. He couldn't figure out why someone who had been hurt would go out every night. Unless... "Shit!"

Locky raced down the steps, taking them two at a time. He flung open the front door and studied the dark streets, searching for a glimpse of Becket, nothing, not even a passing car. How could he have disappeared so quickly?

Walking back into the house, Locky sought out Charlie and Jack. He found them in the kitchen finishing the dishes. "I thought that was Chase's job?"

Jack chuckled. "It was, but one of his friends called" —he gestured to Charlie— "and ole softy here told him he could go out."

"Give the kid a break," Charlie said in his own defence. "He'll only be young once."

"Speaking of, Becket left. Do either of you have any ideas of where he goes every night?" Locky usually enjoyed the banter between Charlie and Jack, but he had Becket on the brain and knew he wouldn't rest until he figured out what was going on with him.

"No," Charlie answered. "He never says." He took a freshly washed pot from Jack and began to dry it. "Maybe he's going to Fallon's new club."

"Fallon has a club?" *Jesus*. Locky had hoped Fallon Bennett would tire of the small college town and go back to his millions.

"He won't be there," Jack interrupted. "I tried to get him to go with us to Fallon's opening, but he wanted no part of it."

The old Becket would have jumped at the chance to attend the opening. None of it made sense to Locky. The best explanation for Becket's odd behaviour was something Locky hated to even consider. "Do you think he has something going on with Fallon? Maybe he knew the two of you wouldn't approve, so he thought it best to stay away from him in your presence."

Jack shook his head. "We told him to stay away from Fallon."

"And has he?" Locky doubted it.

"I don't know," Jack admitted. "Like we said before, he won't talk to us anymore about anything other than his job."

Just like that, Locky knew the truth. Hell, he'd practically pushed Becket into Fallon's arms after the kiss they'd shared months earlier. Although it had been the best kiss of his life, Locky knew he'd end up getting his heart broken if he put his faith into Becket.

So, like the asshole Becket believed him to be, he'd pushed Becket away. "Where's Fallon's place?"

* * * *

From his hiding place in the alley behind Fallon's club, Becket sat on the milk crate he'd swiped from the grocery store down the street and settled in for another long shift of watching. Since setting up his nightly vigil, he'd seen more dark alley blow jobs than he cared to think about.

Through the open curtains upstairs, he'd seen Fallon fuck a different guy every night, but had yet to see one of them so out of it they had to be carried away like he had. Jigger, on the other hand, had helped more than one twink into his car after the bar closed. Was Jigger the one who had drugged him or was the man just a pervert who got off on fucking drunk guys who barely looked legal?

Becket had even confronted Jigger a few nights earlier when he'd caught the beefy bartender loading a drunk guy into his car. Unfortunately, the drunk co-ed turned out to be one of the senior football players who offered to rearrange Becket's face if he got in the way of a fuck he'd been working all night on.

Despite the incident, Becket refused to rule Jigger out—he'd even tried talking to the bartender again the following night. Unfortunately, that didn't turn out so well. Jigger had threatened to call the cops and lodge a formal complaint if Becket ever accused him of something so heinous again.

Becket had considered going to the police himself, but then he'd have to tell someone what he'd allowed to happen and why he'd gone to Fallon's in the first place. Worst of all, Locky would find out.

Becket may have accepted the fact that his attraction to Locky was one-sided, but he hadn't been able to get the man out of his system, and although he hated to admit it, he still cared. "Stupid feelings," he mumbled.

Deep in thought, Becket jumped when his cell phone rang. He dug into his pocket but not before the ringing surprised two would-be gropers. "Sorry," he called out to the two men before glancing at the display.

"Hey, Mom," Becket answered.

"Sorry, it's not Carrie, it's Lisa."

Lisa? Becket couldn't remember his brother Nic's wife ever calling him. The fact that she was phoning from his parents' house filled him with dread. "What's going on? Did something happen with Mom?"

"Your dad's had a heart attack. We were all eating dinner together and he just collapsed at the table. Nic started CPR and Cade called for an ambulance…"

"Is he dead?" Becket got to his feet. He should've stayed in Iowa. If he hadn't let his need for sex lure him to Idaho, he would've been there at his father's side. More importantly, Becket would've been at his mother's side, helping her deal with the situation.

"No, he's alive, but they're transferring him to Des Moines." Lisa cleared her throat. "He needs a quadruple bypass, but they're not sure he's strong enough to survive the surgery."

"Tell Mom I'm using the emergency credit card she gave me to get the first flight out. I'll be there as soon as I can." Becket left his hiding place behind as he started down the alley. "I'll fly into Des Moines and get a cab to the hospital."

"Hurry. Carrie needs you." Lisa made a noise that sounded like a forced laugh. "She has all of us here, but she keeps asking about you. I always suspected you were her favourite, now I guess I have proof."

Becket was the baby, and his brothers often accused him of being the favourite, but he knew the truth of why his mom needed him home. He alone knew the secret his mom needed him home to help hide from the others. "Naw, she just wants everyone together. I'll call you when I get to the airport."

Becket hung up and shoved the phone in his pocket. He took off towards BK determined to get to his mom's side no matter what it took. Worrying about himself, or what was going on inside Fallon's club or bedroom, was no longer his top priority.

* * * *

Locky pushed and excused his way through the packed crowd, searching for a glimpse of Becket. While he spotted a few familiar faces, none of them belonged to the man he was looking for. Closer to the bar, he noticed Fallon. Surrounded by men, Fallon laughed it up like he didn't have a care in the world.

Locky quickly scanned the men and, while some of them were quite handsome, none of them were Becket. He caught Fallon's attention, and with a few spoken words the guys drifted off.

"How can I help you this evening?" Fallon asked, mistrust running heavily through his tone.

"I'm looking for Becket," Locky simply replied.

"Haven't seen him in a while. He came by a couple of weeks ago, but I was busy so I asked him to wait for me. That's the last I've seen of him. Called him a few times, but he never answers or returns my messages." Fallon took a sip of his drink and smiled. "Why the sudden interest in Becket?"

An accusation was on the tip of Locky's tongue, but the lawyer in him prevailed. "I don't know what really happened when he was here last, but he's not been the same since. Did you know he broke his hand punching a wall?"

"No, I didn't. I'm sorry to hear that, but like I said, I haven't seen or spoken to him."

Although Locky still didn't trust Fallon, the concern in Fallon's expression appeared to be genuine. "Call BK House if he comes in, will ya?"

"Of course." Fallon gestured to the bar. "Can I buy you a drink?"

"No thanks. Remember to call if you see him," Locky told Fallon before pushing his way back through the crowd. He stood on the sidewalk in front of the bar and pulled out his phone.

"BK," Charlie answered.

"He's not at Fallon's," Locky said, climbing behind the wheel of his car.

"No, he's not. He just left with Jack headed for the airport."

"Airport? Where the hell's he going now?" Locky's head spun with the sudden turn of events.

"His dad's had a heart attack. Becket's flying back to Iowa."

"For how long?" Locky still didn't know what had happened to Becket, but he hoped his father's illness wasn't giving him an excuse to drop out of college.

"He didn't say. His flight isn't until six, but he didn't want Jack to have to wake up at four to get him there on time when he can just sleep in one of the chairs at the airport." Charlie cleared his throat. "Of course it could also have something to do with the fact that Jack told him you went out looking for him."

Locky hated the thought of Becket sitting alone at the airport all night. "Do you think I should go talk to him?"

"He's got a jump on you. Hell, he'd probably already be through security by the time you got there."

"I could always buy a ticket to get through security," Locky suggested.

"Sounds like a waste of money to me. Why would you do that?"

Locky made a sharp left turn and headed for the airport. "I don't really know. Maybe I care more than I've admitted to."

* * * *

Slumped down in a chair, Becket was startled awake when someone sat right beside him. He opened his eyes, prepared to defend himself and came face to face with Locky. "What're you doing here?"

Locky held up his ticket. "I'm going to Des Moines to sit with a friend."

Becket narrowed his gaze and tried to reconcile the man beside him with the one who'd pushed him away only a few months earlier. "Why would you do that?"

Locky shrugged. "Because despite what you think, I care. I know you're struggling with something, and I'd like to be there for you in case you ever feel like talking about it."

"I won't," Becket warned him. He glanced at Locky. Why did the man have to be so damn handsome? "Sorry you wasted your money."

"I didn't." Locky chuckled. "Although, I wasn't really planning on going to Iowa when I left the house, so I'm going to have to do some shopping."

Becket wasn't sure what to think of Locky's decision to follow him home. Would Locky try to pressure him into talking? He got up and walked over to stand in front of the wall of windows. The airstrip was empty, luggage carts idle, ready to resume another busy workday in a few short hours. He should tell Locky to go home, back to BK, but he longed to spend time with him no matter the circumstance.

Becket turned back to gaze at the hot guy who sat patiently several feet away. "I'm from a really small town."

"I think you told me that before," Locky replied.

"I might've, but I probably didn't mention that I'm not *out* in Crescent Ridge. I mean, my family knows, but it's not the kind of thing you announce to a town where gossip is the most popular pastime. I knew I was leaving as soon as I graduated, so my folks thought it best that I kept my sexuality under wraps."

Locky shifted in the chair. "I'm just trying to be a good friend, here. There's no reason your family or anyone else should know either of us are gay." He glanced up at Becket, giving him that sexy as hell grin that always made Becket's knees feel like rubber. "Unless you've got an older brother that looks like you and swings our way?"

Becket laughed. He should probably feel affronted, but it was an old argument between the two of them. Still, the thought of Locky flirting with one of his corn-fed, macho brothers was too funny. "I'd like to see that."

"You're sick."

Becket flopped back into the chair beside Locky. "I have three brothers, Cade, Nic and Del. They're all over six-foot, broad as a barn and married to their high school sweethearts. You're hot, but I don't think even *you* could sway one of my brothers to our side."

Locky stretched his arms over his head and yawned. "I'm too tired to seduce anyone anyway. I guess the state of Iowa will be safe for now."

When Locky closed his eyes, Becket took the opportunity to study the man who visited his dreams each night. Goddamn, Locky was hot—beyond hot—scorching. His gaze travelled to the crotch of Locky's jeans. He'd felt the hard press of that impressive cock the one and only time Locky had kissed him.

Becket looked around the near-empty terminal. The lights had been dimmed and a few travellers were asleep in chairs or stretched out on the floor along the walls, but it seemed no one was paying him and Locky any attention. It would be so easy to reach down and feel the bulge in Locky's jeans.

Locky cleared his throat, drawing Becket's attention away from his cock. Staring at him with those light green eyes, the corner of Locky's mouth turned up. "Don't even think about it."

"About what? I'm just sitting here." Becket gave Locky the innocent expression that had always worked like a charm on his mom.

"Yeah, you're just sitting there staring at my dick," Locky mumbled. The accusation was right on, but Becket didn't detect a trace of anger in Locky's smooth, deep voice.

"Guilty," Becket confessed, "but you can't blame a guy. I mean, it's right there tempting me."

Locky bumped his shoulder against Becket's. "Get some sleep."

"Do you mind if I dream about your cock?"

Locky chuckled. "Many do."

Chapter Three

Locky dropped Becket at the hospital entrance before making a quick run to the nearest mall. He picked up a cheap duffle bag and four changes of clothes, including a bag of personal items from the local drugstore.

The shopping was easy, but explaining to Charlie why he felt the need to follow Becket all the way to Iowa had been more difficult. He knew when he'd bought the ticket he was showing his hand, maybe not to Becket, but to himself, Jack and Charlie.

Locky's plan had been to offer Becket a shoulder to lean on and hopefully win his trust, but keeping his head around him became harder with every moment he spent in Becket's company.

Catching a glimpse of himself in the rental car's rear view mirror, Locky scowled. He'd been burnt before, and he'd vowed never again to put his trust in someone too young to know what they really wanted out of life. "Don't fall into that trap again," he warned his reflexion.

"Are you coming up or were you planning to talk to yourself the rest of the day?"

Locky had been so deep in thought he hadn't even noticed Becket approach the car. He was embarrassed that he'd been caught talking to himself, but he refused to acknowledge it. "It's not too bad here in the shade. I figured I'd give you all time alone."

"Yeah, well, I told them you came with me, and now they think you don't want to meet them." Becket folded his arms and rested them on the door while he talked through the open window. "Cade even said to tell you he didn't bite, which is like saying you're already family."

Locky smiled. He seemed to do that a lot around Becket, and it felt damn good after a summer spent with his stuffy parents. "Fine. Get off the door so I can roll up the window."

Becket stepped back and waited for Locky to join him. "You get everything you needed?"

Locky secured the car. "Just about. I thought I'd rent a room across the street, but I figured I should talk to you first."

"I doubt we'll need a room. Dad's out of surgery, and as soon as he's stable, mom needs us to go to the farm and take care of a few things there."

"I could still rent a room. That way if you're family needed a shower or a break they could just go across the street."

Becket tilted his chin up and shielded his eyes from the sun as he met Locky's gaze. "You'd do that for them?"

"Of course," Locky sighed. He hated that Becket took Locky's refusal to get involved sexually to mean he didn't care. "I'm not the asshole you think I am."

Hands stuffed into the front pockets of his jeans, Becket stopped walking before they reached the front door. "I know you're a good guy. Why do you think I like you so much? Your cock's big, but I'm not stupid enough to believe that's enough."

The statement surprised Locky. Although it was nice to know Becket thought he was more than a great lay, Locky didn't like the direction the conversation was headed. He put his hand on Becket's shoulder and urged him forward. "Come on, it's time I met your family."

"Don't let my brothers intimidate you," Becket warned as they entered the hospital.

"I was raised by the king of intimidation, don't worry about me." Locky gestured for Becket to precede him into the elevator. On the ride up, he studied Becket. "Do they think your dad'll be okay?"

Becket nodded. "My dad's a bull. If he had his way, he'd be outta here tomorrow and in the field. Luckily, despite his size, my mom secretly wears the pants in the family." He chuckled. "Don't tell him I told you that though."

"My lips are sealed," Locky agreed.

The elevator doors opened and Locky followed Becket to a small waiting room outside the ICU. Becket hadn't exaggerated his brothers' stature. As each one introduced himself, Locky held out his hand in greeting.

Cade, the oldest brother, gave Locky a narrow-eyed gaze as they shook hands. "Pardon me, but you look a little old to still be in school."

Locky knew his age would come up, so he wasn't surprised. "I'm in charge of student life at the house where Becket lives. I graduated from Stanford with a law degree four years ago, but found working the profession wasn't as rewarding as I'd hoped."

Locky didn't go into what had really prompted him to leave his old life in search of something that held meaning. His memories from that night in the parking lot were his to deal with, and he thought he'd done a fairly good job on his own.

"So part of your job is to accompany the students when they're called home for an emergency?" Cade continued to question.

Locky tried to maintain his composure despite the obvious challenge. "I came because I was concerned for Becket."

"Leave him alone, Cade," a female said, coming into the room.

Locky knew by the way Cade stepped back and lowered his gaze that he was in the presence of the matriarch of the Chandler family. Dressed in a pair of blue jeans and a short-sleeved button up blouse, Mrs Chandler approached.

"It's nice to finally meet you." Instead of shaking Locky's hand, she hugged him.

Unfamiliar with parental affection, Locky wasn't sure what to do at first but eventually settled his hands on the older woman's back. "It's nice to meet you as well, Mrs Chandler."

"Call me Carrie." She released him and shook her head. "You certainly are as handsome as Becket described you."

"Mom!" Becket yelled, louder than was prudent in a hospital.

Locky glanced at Becket and couldn't help but smile. Face red and mouth set in a grim line, Becket looked like he wanted to strangle his mother. "It's okay."

"No, it's not," Becket said, with genuine hurt in his voice. He turned to look pleadingly at his mom. "I talked to you in confidence. I can't believe you just said that."

Carrie brushed Becket's cheek with the palm of her hand. "I'm so sorry, it slipped out." She wrapped her son in her arms and hugged him close. "Please forgive me?"

There was something so poignant about the moment that Locky had to fight back tears. He noticed the other brothers were already heading back to their seats like nothing had ever happened. Was such a profound moment between mother and son so commonplace they couldn't see the beauty in it? Normal or not, Locky had never shared anything like it with his mother.

"Of course I do." Becket returned his mom's affection. "Just don't spill anymore of my secrets."

Leaving mother and son to their embrace, Locky moved away and sat by the others. After a few seconds, Becket released his mom and walked over to Locky. "Do you mind if I leave you to the animals while I take mom down to the cafeteria to get her something to eat?"

"Not at all." Locky wasn't sure how he'd fill the time, but he supposed he could try to get to know Becket's family.

"I won't be long," Becket assured Locky. He leant forward and whispered in Locky's ear. "She hasn't eaten since dinner and she won't unless I guilt her into it."

"I understand. I'll be fine." Locky reached for a magazine on a nearby table. "I'll just read or something."

"Thanks." Becket joined his mom and led her from the room.

Del nudged Locky with his elbow and gestured to Becket and Carrie. "Sickening, isn't it? She's always treated him like a baby."

Sickening wasn't how Locky would describe it, and part of him resented Becket's brother for seeing it that way. "He's the youngest," Locky replied in Becket's defence, "of course Carrie would treat him that way."

Del shook his head. "We were all glad when he went away to school. We thought it would help both of them." He looked at his other brothers as if searching for permission to speak further. "We lost our only sister to Sudden Infant Death Syndrome before Becket was born. It nearly destroyed Mom, nearly destroyed our family, but when she got pregnant with Becket, she was so happy that we thought she was going to be okay..."

Del suddenly stopped talking, and Locky was left to wonder why he'd cut himself off. "She seemed fine to me," Locky finally added.

"She is, in most areas, but she's smothered Becket his entire life and he's allowed it," Cade said, adding his two cents to the conversation.

Lisa made an exasperated sound and pointed her finger at Cade. "What do you guys expect? The three of you have scared the crap out of Becket by telling him about the way she was after she lost Abby."

"If we told him anything it was years ago," Cade argued with his sister-in-law. "He's a grown man now, and he and Mom need to face up to the fact that he's not her baby any longer."

Locky held his tongue. It was obviously an ongoing argument between family members that was none of his business. He thought of the way Becket acted at

BK and couldn't reconcile the brothers' version of their younger brother with the man he knew. Sure, Becket was young and in some areas still immature, but he was only twenty. What did Cade and Del see in Becket that Locky didn't?

* * * *

"I'm sorry if I embarrassed you," Carrie said between spoonfuls of tomato soup.

"It's okay, Mom." Becket picked at the cast on his hand. "He's not here because he likes me like that. I wish he did, but he doesn't."

"Then why would he come?"

Becket pushed the grilled cheese sandwich closer to her, prompting without words for her to eat. The last person in the world who needed to know what had happened to him that night was his mother, so it was hard to explain Locky's concern without telling on himself. "When I got the call about Dad I was pretty upset. Part of Locky's job is to make sure the residents at BK are doing okay, so I guess that's why he offered to come."

"Well it was very nice of him." She reached over and touched Becket's cast. "I worry about you living so far from home. It's nice to know you have someone looking out for you."

Becket wished he had Locky fucking him, not looking out for him, but he wasn't about to spill those beans. "Locky's going to rent a hotel room across the street. He thought it would be a good place for you, and whoever else stays, to shower and get some sleep without getting too far from Dad."

"He doesn't need to do that. Your father and I have money to do that if we need to." Carrie took a bite of her sandwich before making a disgusted face. "How could they possibly mess up a grilled cheese?" She shook her head and pushed the sandwich to the side before going back to her soup.

While Becket knew his parents had the money for a hotel room, he also knew his mom would never spend it on something she would consider so frivolous. "Well, too late," he lied, "he's already rented and paid for it."

"Well you remind me when we get back upstairs, and I'll write him a check."

Again, Becket felt justified to lie. "Okay, but I think it'll hurt his feelings." He shrugged. "It's his way of helping."

Carrie set her spoon down. "I don't want to do that." She tapped her short fingernails on the table. "Maybe I can come up with another way to pay him back."

Pleased with himself, Becket smiled. "I'm sure you'll think of something."

Carrie loaded her dishes onto the tray and got to her feet. "We'd better get back up there."

"Sure." Becket took the tray from his mom.

Carrie pointed to Becket's cast. "I've also spoken to your father's doctor about getting another x-ray on that."

"I don't think a cardiologist is the right person to see about a broken hand. Besides, the doctor I saw at school was a real one, so I trust him." He set the tray back onto the table after looking around for a place to put it. "I think we're supposed to just leave this on the table."

"You can't always trust doctors," Carrie warned with a shake of her finger. "They told me Abby was a healthy baby."

As far as Becket was aware, it had been three years since his mom had spoken Abby's name. He braced himself for her predictable, yet sad, reaction. "You wanna stop by the chapel?"

"No, I don't think we have time. Abby's probably upstairs waiting for us." Carrie pulled away and headed for the elevator.

"Wait." Becket caught up with his mom. "I really want you to go sit with me in the chapel for a few minutes."

Becket had spent years covering for his mom's lapses in sanity and had only agreed to go to college once he felt assured she was better. He supposed his father's frail condition had prompted the memories that continued to haunt his mom nearly twenty-four years after Abby's death, but the setback could be disastrous for Becket's chances of returning to school.

"What about Abby?" Carrie asked, resisting Becket's efforts to get her to the chapel.

"She'll understand, Mom."

At last, Carrie succumbed to Becket's wish and followed him. "Just a few minutes."

Becket remembered the first time his brothers had told him about their mom's breakdown after Abby's death and how she would go days talking to a child that was no longer alive. It was just after one of his mom's lapses, and Nic, Cade and Del were worried she would have to go back into the psychiatric hospital. At the time, Becket didn't even know what a psychiatric hospital was, so he'd asked his teacher. She'd looked at him with compassion in her eyes, obviously knowing the family history, and explained, in kid-friendly detail, what it was. Becket had made up his mind to do whatever it took to make sure his mom never had to go away again. It hadn't been easy and at times he felt guilty for deceiving his family, but because he was his mother's baby, easing her back to reality seemed to come more naturally to him.

Becket was grateful the chapel was empty and guided his mom to one of the small pews. Only big enough to seat around sixteen people, the space was quiet and tranquil, with muted overhead lighting and candles flickering through the room. It usually took several minutes for his mom to return to normal, so it was the perfect spot for them to hide.

"Pretty," his mom commented.

"Yes," Becket agreed, sitting beside her. He tried to think of something to say to bring his mother back to reality. "I can't wait to see Locky try to help me with the chores. I doubt he's ever been on a farm." He chuckled. "It'll be an eye-opening experience for him, I bet."

"Go easy on him, and whatever you do, don't laugh if he makes a mistake." She squeezed Becket's hand. "Men hate that, especially men who are used to being good at everything they do."

Becket rested his head against his mom's shoulder. "Do you think he's too old for me?"

"It's not about age. It's about what you both want out of life that matters. You're young, and I'm sure there are plenty of things that you still want to do that he's already done." Carrie ruffled Becket's curls. "You have plenty of life ahead of you, baby, don't rush it."

Becket wished he could talk to his mom about the night at Fallon's. The sense of betrayal he still felt daily was starting to eat away at everything he considered good about himself.

They sat in silence for several moments before his mom spoke. "It happened again, didn't it?"

Becket nodded. "It didn't last long. I think dad has you really worried, but he'll be okay." He kissed his mom's cheek. "I love you."

"I love you too. I miss you when you're gone, but I understand why you needed to leave."

* * * *

Locky followed Becket's directions out of Des Moines, headed west on I-80. He had a million questions swimming around in his head, but he was afraid to voice any of them. It had been obvious to everyone in the waiting room that something was…off when Becket and Carrie had returned from lunch.

"You're quiet," Becket said, staring at Locky. "Did my brothers give you a hard time?"

"No." Locky cleared his throat, hoping to dislodge the foremost thought on his mind. "They told me about Abby."

Becket immediately looked away from Locky to stare out of the passenger window. "They shouldn't have done that."

"Don't get mad at them. I think they were just trying to explain why you and your mom are so close." Locky could tell from Becket's body language that the conversation made him uneasy. His usual sprawl gone, Becket was drawing in on himself, practically hugging the side door. "We don't have to talk about it. I was just answering your question."

"Mom needs me, and more than likely, I won't be going back to school," Becket mumbled. "I don't like it, but it is what it is."

Locky took the next exit he came to, pulled the rental car to the side of the off ramp, and parked. "Don't do that. You have three brothers living within a mile of your folks. Let them help out more if your parents need it. Go back, get your education and then decide what's best for your family. This is your time. Allow yourself to have it."

"It's not that easy."

Locky reached across the seat and rested his hand on Becket's shoulder. "You're twenty. It should be exactly that easy."

"Did my brothers tell you that my dad put Mom into a nut house after Abby died?"

The question surprised Locky. "No, they said she had some problems that nearly destroyed your family, but they didn't give specifics."

"Yeah, well, Dad's good at one thing, farming. Don't get me wrong, I know he loves us and Mom, but when she got sick after Abby died, he stuck her in a hospital so he wouldn't have to worry about her being at home with Nic, Del and Cade while he worked the fields." Becket shook his head. "It's always been about the fields."

It wasn't Locky's place to comment on a family he knew so little about, but he couldn't stay quiet. "Not to play devil's advocate, but your dad had an entire farm to run as well as three small children to take care of. I imagine he felt overwhelmed at the time, and getting your mom the help she obviously needed was one thing he knew would help the situation."

"Or maybe he just didn't wanna be bothered?" Becket turned in the seat to face Locky. "Her lapses don't last long, and even if they did, so what? She's not dangerous to herself or anyone else. So, maybe she has moments when she thinks Abby is still alive. Why is that so horrible that the answer is to put her away? And don't think Dad wouldn't have done it again if he'd known she continued to have them, because he would have in a second, and I knew it."

Locky felt the pain and anger radiating from Becket and wondered how many years he had kept both feelings locked inside. "She still has them?"

"She had one today. That's why we were gone so long when I took her to lunch."

"How can the rest of your family not know?" Locky felt compelled to reach out and cup Becket's cheek. Everything he thought he knew about Becket was proving to be wrong.

"I think some part of Mom feels safe with me because she knows I'll love her no matter what. Besides, no one else is really around her during the day. Farmers are the hardest working people I know. Dad wakes with the sun, works 'til sunset and is in bed an hour after he eats supper."

Becket leaned into Locky's touch. "I'm sure Mom spends many afternoons talking to Abby like she was still with us, but no one's there to see it. I know that in the past, she did better during the winter months when Dad was inside more. Fuck, who knows, the whole thing might have something to do with her feeling so lonely."

Locky still couldn't wrap his mind around the situation. He understood what loneliness could do to a person, hell, just look at his mother for example. Gloria Regent was a wealthy woman whose husband spent the majority of their marriage either at the office or in the courtroom, and as a result, she became mean and bitter towards everyone, including her only child. From what he'd witnessed, Locky agreed with Becket's opinion about his mother. Carrie seemed happy and loving despite the cards life had dealt. Of course, he'd never witnessed one of her 'lapses', as

Becket called them, but from Locky's understanding, they didn't seem to hurt anyone.

Locky moved his hand from Becket's cheek to the back of his neck. "Can I kiss you?"

Becket's dark eyebrows drew together. "Why?"

"Because I want to more than anything," Locky finally admitted, giving in to his need for the first time in months.

Becket's hesitance reminded Locky of why he'd accompanied the younger man to Iowa in the first place. The last thing Becket needed was to feel pressured. He withdrew his hand. "I'm sorry. I had no right to ask."

Becket just sat there for several moments before unbuckling his seatbelt and launching himself over the centre console. He wrapped his arms around Locky's neck and pressed their lips together.

With a groan of appreciation, Locky blindly moved his seat back and settled Becket in his lap. Fuck, he'd dreamt of tasting Becket again but had held himself back, too afraid to get involved. Becket's tongue duelled expertly with Locky's, showing experience Locky didn't want to think about.

Locky slid his hands down to cup Becket's ass, wishing they were anywhere but on the off-ramp. Becket tried to readjust to give Locky better access and ended up smacking his cast against the back of Locky's head.

Becket immediately pulled back. "Shit, I'm sorry."

With his lips still tingling and his dick throbbing, Locky smiled. "Don't be. I needed something to cool me off anyway." He rested his head against the back of the seat. "How much further?"

"An hour, give or take." Becket swiped his tongue across Locky's lower lip. "It was even better than I remembered."

"Yeah," Locky agreed.

After several more teasing kisses, Becket moved back to the passenger seat and buckled up. "Are you going to regret that?"

"I don't know," Locky said in honesty. "Guess that depends on you and why you let me kiss you."

"What the hell's that supposed to mean? I've wanted you since your first day at BK, and I've never been shy about letting you know." Becket adjusted his cock.

Locky didn't want to get into why he'd always rebuffed Becket's advances, but he needed him to understand where he was coming from. "It's never been because I don't want you. Christ Almighty, I think the opposite is true, but that's what scares the hell out of me. You're young."

Becket opened his mouth, ready to defend himself, but Locky held up his hand. "Let me finish. You're young, and I don't in any way fault you because of that, but I've been burned before because someone wanted to use me as a teacher so he could move on to fucking the entire city."

"Pretty sure of your skills, are ya?"

Locky realised how his statement sounded and laughed. "Yeah, I guess I am."

Becket put his feet up on the dash and crossed his legs at the ankles. "Maybe I have my own skills. Maybe you'll be the one to learn something."

Moments after the light-hearted words were out of Becket's mouth, Locky noticed an abrupt change in his expression. *Shit.* The sweet, loving son who arrived in Iowa had suddenly transformed into the sullen man he'd worried about at BK House. Locky had promised that he wouldn't push, but he couldn't let go without saying something. "I don't know what happened, but I wish you'd let me help you."

With his head down, Becket sat silent for several minutes. "I went out. Had a drink. Someone fucked me without a condom and dumped me on the porch." He turned his head and met Locky's gaze. "That's it."

Locky's initial concern was for Becket's health. "Have you seen a doctor?"

Becket bobbed his head up and down lazily. "Had a whole round of tests run. I have to go back in a couple months for more." He fisted his hands. "I tried taking the medication the doctor gave me just in case whoever fucked me had HIV, but I couldn't handle the side effects and still keep Charlie and Jack in the dark."

Whoever? Locky's breath caught in his chest. His worst fear about what had happened to Becket was realised. "You were raped."

"Raped? No. That part was my fault. I went out that night wanting to get fucked and that's exactly what I got. The only problem is I think I was drugged, so I don't know by who or how."

Anger began to build within Locky. "Tell me where you were when it happened." He had a good idea, but he needed to hear it from Becket. There had to be a reason Becket refused to return Fallon's calls or visit his new club. The old Becket would have made a place like Fallon's on Fifth a weekly haunt.

Becket shook his head. "That's all I'm saying. I don't know who did it, and I won't accuse someone by mistake."

"You need to go to the police." Locky tried to reach for Becket's hand, but Becket pulled away before Locky could touch him.

"I told you what happened, now drop it."

"I don't think I can," Locky confessed. "Not when I know it could happen to someone else."

Becket turned away from Locky to stare out of the passenger window once more. "It hasn't. I've seen him leave with other guys who went willingly. I actually had a moment of insanity and confronted him about it."

"Who do you think is watching tonight?" Locky was pushing Becket too hard and he knew it, but Becket needed to face up to the true crime against him.

"Fuck!" Becket threw open the door and got out of the car. Although they were parked on the side of the off-ramp, the ground sloped down sharply beyond the pavement and within two steps, Becket lost his balance, pitching him down the hill.

Locky checked for traffic before jumping out and going around the trunk of the car to check on Becket. Halfway down the embankment, Becket was lying on his back with his casted arm to one side and his left arm over his eyes. Sideways, Locky eased his way down the slope. "Are you hurt?"

Locky's chest constricted when Becket didn't move or answer him. He scrambled faster, finally reaching the supine man. "Becket?"

"I'm not there. What if he does it again?" Becket's voice was so soft Locky barely heard the words.

Locky laid his hand on Becket's chest. "Are you hurt?" he asked again.

"Just my pride, what little I still have of it," Becket answered.

"I know you're afraid of going to the police, but you can't take on the burden of watching whoever it is you're watching twenty-four hours a day. It's not fair to you or anyone else who might get hurt." Locky uncovered Becket's eyes and gazed down at him. "Even if you went out looking for a good time, you didn't give anyone permission to drug you or fuck you. That's a crime, and whoever did it will do it again if someone doesn't stop him."

"There's no evidence. Even if I went to the police, I can't tell them who did it."

Locky leant down and gave Becket a gentle kiss on the lips before pulling back. "Maybe not, but you can tell them where you were when it happened. That should narrow it down. If nothing else, it'll make the police aware of a predator they may not know about."

"I'll think about it." Becket looked around. "We'd better get to the farm before we lose the light."

Chapter Four

Becket tore the note off the screen door and passed it back to Locky. "Scotty Melbourne, Cade's best friend, took care of the animals for us. So you're off the hook, at least for tonight."

Locky read the note while following Becket inside the house. "It says the eggs are in the refrigerator. How'd he get in?"

Becket laughed and threw his duffle bag on the couch. "Through the unlocked door."

Locky set his bag down beside Becket's. "Is this an Iowa thing?"

"No, it's a country thing." Becket glanced over his shoulder. "Hungry? We have eggs."

Locky wrinkled his nose. "Right out of the chicken? No thanks."

Becket couldn't hold back his laughter. "I hate to break it to you, city boy, but they come that way. Or has Portland figured out a way to manufacture them?"

"Hardy har har," Locky mocked. "I just prefer my eggs in a carton from the store."

Becket opened the fridge and searched its contents. "Can you eat ham or does the fact that we have a pig farm down the road gross you out?"

"Give me the damn ham."

Becket handed Locky the package of lunchmeat and retrieved the cardboard carton of eggs before shutting the fridge. "Oh look, ours are in cartons, too."

Locky growled but softened the sound with a grin.. "Are you making fun of me?"

Becket set the eggs on the counter and draped his arms over Locky's shoulders. "Yeah. You gonna do something about it?"

Locky's ham joined Becket's eggs. "Do you want me to?"

Becket rubbed his cast against the front of Locky's jeans. Although he couldn't actually feel anything through the thick plaster, Locky's groan told Becket it was having the desired effect. The sound of Locky's pleasure turned Becket on for the first time since his visit to Fallon's. He shoved thoughts of that night away before they had a chance to ruin the moment. He'd waited too long for Locky, and he refused to let an unknown man spoil his reactions to the kisses Locky was peppering his neck with. Becket turned his head enough so they could brush lips. "Wanna see my bedroom?"

"Are you sure?"

"No," Becket said with honesty, "but I'd like to try." He prayed he didn't make a fool of himself, but, God, he wanted it so much.

* * * *

While Becket used the restroom down the hall, Locky unpacked his newly purchased duffle bag. He found the small plastic bag from the drug store and pulled out the lube and box of condoms. He couldn't stop thinking that what he was contemplating was wrong. Not only was Becket young, but he'd recently gone through a traumatic experience, one that he still hadn't dealt with.

Locky sat on the edge of the mattress and tossed the supplies on the nightstand. "I can't do this," he mumbled.

"They make pills for that," Becket joked, coming into the room with a towel wrapped around his waist. He removed the plastic bread sack off his cast and dropped it in the trashcan.

Riveted by the site of the bulge behind the terrycloth, Locky was temporarily speechless, but when that fantastic bulge came closer, he couldn't deny its effect on his own cock. He spread his legs and reached out to pull Becket between them. "My equipment is in perfect working order. It's my conscience I'm having a hard time with."

Becket released the towel and straddled Locky's lap. Palming the front of Locky's jeans, Becket leant forward. "I'm the one who should be worried, and I'm right here."

Locky settled his hands on Becket's hips, fighting the urge to touch and explore the ass he longed to bury his cock in. "Tell me you're not doing this in an effort to erase that night from your mind?"

"I don't even remember that night, so how can that be the case. Besides, I've hoped for this for a very long time." Becket squeezed Locky's erection. "Tell you what, get undressed and get in bed with me and we'll see just how much I want you." He punctuated the last word with a kiss.

Locky eyed the box of condoms on the table.

"Oh." Becket quickly climbed off Locky's lap. "You're not worried for the reason I thought." He picked the towel up and wrapped it around him, holding it in place with his good hand. "Does it help if I say that the doctor told me it was rare to get HIV after a single night with an unknown partner?"

Shocked by the abrupt change in the situation, it took Locky a few moments to catch up to Becket's train of thought. "What? You think I'm worried about sleeping with you because I'm afraid you'll expose me?" He shook his head vehemently. "No. My hesitancy has absolutely nothing to do with that."

"Then what?" Becket asked. "Is it still the age thing?"

Locky stood and wrapped his arms around Becket. Don't push, he reminded himself. "You still haven't acknowledged that you were raped. I guess I'm worried that..." *Shit.* How did he explain his fear without hurting Becket further?

Becket pushed out of Locky's embrace. "You're blackmailing me? If I tell you I was raped, you'll agree to fuck me?" He grabbed Locky's duffle and threw it at him. "I'll make it easy for you. The guestroom's down the hall."

Locky caught his bag and stared at Becket. He couldn't believe he was getting ready to walk away after finally admitting to himself how much he cared for the younger man. Why was it so important to him that he hear Becket say the word? Never in his life had he begged a man to do anything, but he was about to do just that. "I'm sorry, but I don't want to sleep in the other room. I'd much rather sleep in here, with you."

"Just like that you've changed your mind?"

Locky dropped his bag on the floor. "Yes—No." Frustrated with himself, he ran his fingers through his hair. "I don't know. But all I can think about is holding you, and I'm afraid if I leave this room I'll never again get the chance."

Becket stared straight at Locky without giving any indication as to what he was feeling. After several seconds, Becket dropped his towel and pulled back the covers. "Stay if you want, but I sleep in the nude."

* * * *

Becket woke the following morning with the warmest blanket he'd ever known wrapped around him. He snuggled back against the heat of Locky's torso and the arms around him seemed to automatically tighten. *Cool.*

Becket took a chance and scooted his bare ass closer to Locky's morning wood. He only wished Locky hadn't insisted on wearing sleep pants to bed. Becket reached back and pulled his cheeks apart enough to capture the thick erection between them. Locky's cock was beyond hard, beyond big and holy fuck he wanted it inside him.

"Mmm," Locky moaned in his sleep, grinding against Becket.

Becket wondered if he could make them both come without waking Locky. He closed his eyes and wrapped his left hand around his cock while he continued to move against the stiff prick rubbing his ass.

When Locky's grinding turned into thrusts, Becket had a feeling his hesitant lover was starting to wake. Becket began to jerk his cock in earnest, hoping to finish before Locky realised what he was doing.

"You're playing with fire," Locky grumbled in Becket's ear.

"No I'm not, I'm playing with myself," Becket corrected. He took the opportunity to squeeze his ass cheeks together, giving Locky's cock a pseudo embrace.

Locky nuzzled his face against the side of Becket's neck and continued to move against him. "This isn't fair," Locky continued to grumble. "I can't stop now."

"I don't want you to." Goose bumps broke out on Becket's body as he felt Locky fumble with his sleep pants.

Sliding his bare cock up and down the crevice of Becket's ass, Locky started to pant. "Can't stop. Can't stop," Locky said over and over.

"Awww, fuck!" Becket was the first to come, covering his hand with the warm, thick fluid of his passion.

With a deep growl, Locky went rigid. A split second later, Becket felt the first splash of cum land on his lower back. He grinned, more than satisfied with himself for breaking down Locky's wall, but before he could get too comfortable with the change in their relationship, Locky rolled away from him.

"I can't believe I let that happen." Locky sat up and swung his legs over the side of the bed. "I lost control, which is something I never do."

Before Becket could say anything, Locky stood, pulled his pants up and strode from the room. *So much for basking in the afterglow.* He knew if he gave Locky too much time to think about what had happened, the stubborn fool would start re-erecting that damn wall.

Becket was determined not to let that happen. He wiped himself clean with the sheet before getting out of bed. He found the jeans he'd worn the previous day and slipped them on before going after the infuriating man.

"Locky," he called, walking out of the bedroom. With a plan formulating, he knocked on the closed bathroom door. The shower wasn't running so he knew Locky could hear him. "It's not your fault, it's mine. "

Becket was laying it on a bit thick, but if it worked, he'd keep spreading. "I guess I needed to know you actually wanted me because you think I'm a hot piece of ass and not because you're feeling sorry for me."

The door swung open and a red-faced Locky stared down at him. "Don't you dare trivialise what I feel for you. I followed you here like a damn dog, going against everything my fucking head kept telling me because I could no longer deny that I cared. I didn't know the truth about what happened to you, but I knew you were upset, and I couldn't stand the thought of you dealing with it on your own."

Becket took a step back. He'd wanted Locky for a long time, but in his mind, he never thought he had a chance outside the bedroom. He'd certainly never hoped Locky would go beyond telling him he was a great lay.

The house phone rang before Becket could formulate a response. Talk about being saved by the bell. He decided to take the easy way out for the moment. After he had some time to think about the situation he would feel better prepared to share his own feelings. "I'm sorry, but I need to get that in case it's Mom."

Locky nodded. "I understand."

Becket ran to the phone in his parents' bedroom. "Hello?"

"Hey, Mom's been asking for you," Cade drawled. "Sorry, man, I know she asked you to take care of things for her at the farm, but I think you'd do better here." He cleared his throat. "She, uh, had one of those things. Julie was with her and didn't tell me until this morning, but I guess it was bad. Mom kept asking for you and eventually got pretty nasty with Julie when she said you'd left."

"I'm sorry." Becket seemed to say those words a lot lately, but the thought of his mom having one of her lapses in front of Cade's wife could mean the end of the secret.

"It's not your fault. Anyway, we both think it would be better if you're here. I talked to Nic and Del and they're going to head home today. We all feel you could be of more use here."

"Okay." Becket felt Locky's presence and turned to see him standing in the doorway. "Any word on when Dad will be released?"

"Could be as early as tomorrow. You know Dad, he's already raising hell. 'Goddamn hospital just wants to gouge me for more money'," Cade said, doing his best imitation of their father.

"You're getting way too good at that."

"Yeah, well, I've spent my entire life trying to be just like him. Probably the same reason you're a lot like Mom."

Although Cade said it in a joking manner, Becket couldn't help but take offence. "I didn't have much choice, and you know it. Dad didn't want me around."

"That's bullshit. You belonged to Mom and she let everyone know it, *including* Dad. Face it, brother, you were the chosen one."

"That's not fair," Becket argued.

"Fair or not, you came out on the winning end."

"How do you figure?" Becket asked Cade. He turned his back to Locky, hoping to have it out with his oldest brother without him overhearing.

"Mom loved you enough to let you go to college. You think the rest of us were given that choice?"

Becket had always wondered why his brothers didn't seem to like him, guess he had his answer. "I didn't know you wanted to go to college."

"Well I did, but now's not the time to talk about something that'll never happen."

Cade was fifteen years older than Becket, but there was still time if college was something he was genuinely interested in. He made a mental note to get back to that once their dad was home and things had settled down. His mom was the biggest issue at the moment. "Tell me what Julie told you about Mom's lapse."

"Just that they got on the elevator in the lobby and Mom pushed the button for the maternity ward. When Julie tried to correct her, Mom shoved her against the wall and told her no one was going to keep her away from Abby." Cade sighed. "When they arrived on the floor, Mom went to the viewing window and stood there, just staring at the babies like she actually expected Abby to be one of them. I don't know, Becket, maybe it's her being here that's the problem, but we can't let Dad see her like that."

"So why don't I drive over, pick her up and bring her home?" Becket knew his brother was right. If his mom stayed in Des Moines, his dad would eventually find out she'd never fully recovered from Abby's death. He loved his dad, but he was short-sighted and sometimes cruel when it came to dealing with someone he considered abnormal.

"I doubt she'll leave with him still here," Cade replied.

"I can try." Becket glanced over his shoulder. "I'll be there as soon as I can."

"I'll tell her you're coming."

Becket hung up the phone and turned to Locky and explained what had happened. "I *think* I need to bring her here before Dad catches on to what's happening."

"What *is* happening?"

Becket joined Locky in the doorway, their earlier argument forgotten for the moment. "It's Des Moines, it's Dad..." He shook his head. Two days ago his thoughts had only been on himself and his own problems, but now he had Locky, his mom, his dad and the resentment of his brothers to deal with. *Fuck, I'm only twenty.* "How did I get here?"

"We drove." Locky rested his hands on Becket's shoulders. "Are you okay?"

Becket shook his head again. "I just wanted out of this town, out of this house. A few years to finally feel like a kid. Some time to myself, to explore who I was, what I wanted out of life."

"Becket, you're scaring me. What's wrong?"

Becket stared up at Locky. "My whole life's fucked up. Instead of fixing things, I've spent years putting Band-Aids on all the problems in my life, and suddenly everything's coming unstuck."

Locky led Becket out of the master bedroom to the bathroom. He turned on the shower and handed Becket one of the plastic bags Becket had set on the sink the night before. "It's been a hard morning. Why don't you clean-up, and I'll start breakfast."

The expression on Locky's face threatened to break Becket's heart. Did Locky think he was crazy like his mom? No, despite everything else going on, he refused to allow that to happen. "A couple of years ago, I begged my mom to take me to Des Moines, to a Pride Parade. She was afraid to go behind my dad's back, but I begged her until she finally gave in."

Becket turned off the water. "Mom let me drive that day. She was fine until just outside Des Moines. She was uneasy, anxious. I asked her what was wrong, and she started to cry. She asked me if I was taking her back to the hospital where my father had taken her after Abby died. I told her no, that I would never do that, but she wouldn't believe me. I finally had no choice but to turn around and come back home."

"And you think that's why she's having these lapses?"

"Yeah, I think so. I never told anyone," Becket confessed.

"Maybe it's time you did. I'm not trying to get in the middle of your family business, but it sounds like you've spent your entire life trying to protect her."

"I have," Becket agreed. "She didn't have anyone else."

"She had a husband."

"Dad would've put her in the hospital." Becket couldn't believe that Locky still didn't understand the situation. "We've already gone over this. Most of the time she's fine, and even when she's not, she's just confused and sad. No one seems to understand that but me."

Locky leaned in and kissed Becket softly on the lips. He took the bag out of Becket's hand and slipped it over the cast before securing it with a rubber band. "Shower. I'll make breakfast then we'll go pick up your mom." While he spoke, Locky unzipped Becket's jeans and pushed them down.

"Why're you being so cool about this?" Becket stepped out of his jeans and stood naked in front of Locky.

"Because it's clear to me that we have to get you through this family stuff before we can talk about us."

Locky reached down and brushed Becket's flaccid cock with the back of his hand. "And if I have my way, there will be an us."

* * * *

Locky threaded his fingers through Becket's. They'd been on the road for over an hour and had barely said two words to each other, but he refused to take it personally. In the last twenty-four hours, he'd realised that everything he thought he'd known about Becket had been wrong. For almost a year he'd mistaken Becket's carefree attitude as a sign of immaturity, when in actuality, Locky suspected it had more to do with Becket having been released from the unfair responsibilities he'd carried his entire life.

Locky stole a glance at Becket. He wanted him even more now that he knew the truth. Unfortunately, he also understood why it was so important that Becket allow himself the freedom of youth that most people took for granted. For someone who had been figuratively chained to his mother his entire life, the last thing Becket needed was to settle down with his first real boyfriend, and that didn't even take into account the horrendous wrong he'd suffered at the hands of his unknown rapist.

The closer they got to Des Moines, the lower Locky's spirit sank. He tried to remember the old saying about if you love something set it free. *Love?* No. Love wasn't what Becket needed.

"You okay?" Becket asked.

Locky smiled and brought Becket's hand to his mouth. After a quick kiss, he released it and settled both hands on the wheel. "I'm fine."

It was a lie. Locky's heart was at war with his conscience. He should help Becket through his troubles out of friendship, not as a lover, or else he'd never be able to set him free. "How long do you plan to stay once your dad's released?"

"I don't know. Depends on how Mom is, I guess. Why?"

"Because I think I'll fly back Friday. Students should start showing up this weekend, and it's my job to help them get settled. Do you think you'll be ready to head back with me?"

"I have absolutely no clue whether I'll even get to go back."

Locky gripped the steering wheel tighter in an effort to keep from reaching for Becket. "If what you say is true, your mom should be much better once you get her home. Please don't give up on what you've started at school. This is your time, and you've earned it."

"Not according to my brother," Becket grumbled.

Locky hadn't mentioned the obvious argument Becket and his brother got into over the phone, but since Becket brought it up, Locky felt compelled to say something. "You can't take responsibility for your brother, only yourself."

"And my mom," Becket added. "I know you think I'm stupid for doing what I do, but I love her and she's the only one who's ever really loved me back."

Locky knew that wasn't true but it wasn't the time to correct Becket. He was about to say something that Becket wouldn't want to hear. "I think your mom should see a counsellor. I'm not suggesting she's crazy or needs to be put back in the hospital, but I think she needs help in order to deal with what happened. I know you've tried to protect her, but you've done your part. It's time for you to move on with your life and for someone else to step in."

When Becket didn't immediately fire back at him, Locky began to worry. "You hate me for saying that?" Locky asked.

"No, I've been telling myself that for a long time, but knowing it and doing it are two different things."

"Why don't you start by talking to your mom? Ask her if she would consider going to see someone." Locky gave in to his desire and reached for Becket's hand. "It's worth a try, right?"

"Yeah, maybe."

Chapter Five

"This is a nice room, Mom." Becket took a running leap and jumped onto the bed like he'd done when he was a kid.

"The boys rented the one next door last night. It felt nice to have them close again. I know they only live down the road, but it's not the same as when all four of you were home."

Becket held out his hand. "Come over here and sit by me."

After kicking off her shoes and removing Becket's with a tsking sound only mothers can make, his mom laid down beside him. On her back, she stared up at the ceiling. "They told you, didn't they?"

"Yes." Becket rolled to his side and rested his cheek on his mother's shoulder. "I don't want to go back to school with you like this, Mom. But I don't want to stay here either."

"It's not something I can control," she whispered.

"I know." Becket draped his casted hand over his mom and hugged her. "I love you more than I've ever loved anyone, but I don't know how to help you anymore. Maybe it's time we find you someone who can."

"Everyone will know. What if your dad finds out?"

"Is that the problem? Are you really afraid of Dad? He loves you, Mom. I know he doesn't always show it, but I have to believe he does." Becket thought of what Locky had said as an outsider looking in. "I know he really hurt you when he put you away after Abby died, but I think he didn't know what else to do. Abby was his baby, too, and suddenly he was trying to mourn her death and take care of Del, Nic and Cade while worrying about you and how he was supposed to get the farm work done. Maybe trying to get you the help he thought you needed and he couldn't give, was the best he was capable of at the time."

"Why're you taking his side?" Becket's mom rolled away from him.

"I'm not. Locky said…"

"Locky!" she screeched. "Now you're listening to someone who's no better than a stranger to the family!"

"Stop it." Becket jerked back. "Locky's trying to help."

"No!" She swung her legs over the side of the bed and sat up. "He's trying to take you away from me."

With a heavy heart, Becket got off the bed and went to kneel in front of his mom. "No one can take me away from you." He searched for the right words to make her understand. "I'll always be your son, but this is about you. I need you to get better, and I don't think you can do that until you talk to someone about Abby's death."

"I don't talk about that," she said, shaking her head.

"I know, but I think it's time you did. Maybe it'll help."

"No." Becket's mother pulled away and picked up her shoes. "I need to get back to the hospital." She grabbed Becket's sneakers and handed them to him. "Come on."

It was a typical move by his mother. She always bailed when she was uncomfortable with a situation, but this one was too important for Becket to drop. "Don't do that, Mom. You can't keep pretending. *I* can't keep pretending. I'm sorry Abby died, and I've spent my entire life trying to make up for the pain you carry inside, but I can't keep doing it."

"So don't. Go back to school with your new friend and forget all about it. I'll deal with it on my own."

She started for the door, and Becket knew he had one chance to stop her. "I'm going back on Friday. I'd like to help you find a doctor before I go."

"Not necessary. You can go back now if you want. I'd hate to waste anymore of your life."

She walked out without another word, leaving a confused Becket behind. With exploding anger, Becket threw his shoes against the wall, breaking a tacky landscape picture in the process. Pain radiated up his arm, reminding him that he had yet another set of problems waiting for him at school.

Unwilling to face the rest of the day, Becket pulled back the covers and crawled into bed. His mom had made it perfectly clear that she not only wouldn't go seek help, but also if he left her and went back to college, he'd be labelled a traitor in her eyes.

With a groan of frustration, Becket dug into his pocket and retrieved his phone. Of all the problems he wanted to put off dealing with, Locky wasn't one of them. He'd spent almost the entire ride into Des Moines thinking about the earlier conversation they'd had in the bathroom doorway. Locky had feelings for him, real feelings, it seemed.

"Hey," Locky answered the phone.

"Is my mom back there yet?" Becket huddled under the blanket more out of insecurity than a chill in the air-conditioned room.

"Haven't seen her. How'd it go?"

"It sucked. She walked out." Just the sound of Locky's deep voice helped Becket feel calmer. He wondered if that voice would get even deeper the older Locky became. Fun. He closed his eyes and tried to imagine waking up with that sexy growl every morning.

"I'm sorry."

"Not half as sorry as I am. Can you come over?"

"Already on the way."

* * * *

Crossing the street to the hotel, Locky's phone rang. He pulled it out of his pocket and was surprised to see Charlie's name on the display. "Hey."

"How's Becket?" Charlie asked.

"A lot's going on." Locky refused to share all Becket's family secrets. "If you're calling to see when I'm coming back, I made a reservation for Friday morning. I should be there before dinner."

"Good to know, but that's not the reason I'm calling. There was an article in the paper this morning that I thought you might be interested in. A bartender from Fallon's was arrested and charged with drugging and molesting a student here at the college. Someone in his dorm found him unconscious in the lobby and called the police. Anyway, the evidence eventually led them to the bartender, Paul Williams, but everyone knows him as Jigger."

"Fuck!" Locky walked into the hotel lobby and headed straight for the elevator. "I need to talk to Becket."

"Yeah, I thought you might. Whatever he needs, make sure he knows we're here for him."

"I will. Thanks for letting me know." Locky hung up and stepped into the elevator. After a short ride up, he let himself into the rented room and bolted the door. With the lights off and the curtains drawn, he could barely see his hand in front of his face. "You asleep?"

"No, just lying here trying to figure out what's next."

Locky followed the sound of Becket's voice. "I didn't pass Carrie on the way over. Are you sure she was going back to the hospital?"

"Who knows where she was going. She just walked out, told me to go back to school tonight, that we didn't need to wait until Friday." Becket grabbed Locky's hand as soon as he neared the bed. "Kick your shoes off and get in. Please?"

Locky did as asked. Talking to Becket about his phone call from Charlie was going to be tricky. The last thing he wanted was to plant false memories in Becket's head about what happened that night. Becket scooted against him and he was surprised to feel skin, a lot of it. "What's going on, you were so upset you decided to get naked?"

"Complaining?"

Locky ran his palm down Becket's side to his hip. He tried to keep his mind off sex but he was only human. "I'm confused, not stupid."

"You're also overdressed." Becket clumsily pulled Locky's T-shirt off over his head. "Everything in my life's turned to shit." He kissed Locky's chest. "Except this. You."

Locky's eyes drifted shut as Becket kissed and licked a path down his torso. *Stay strong.* As good as Becket's mouth felt and as badly as he wanted it to continue, he couldn't become the distraction Becket was so obviously looking for. "Did you get your mom to talk about what happened to Abby?"

Becket stopped in the process of unzipping Locky's jeans. "You wanna talk about this now?"

"We *have* to talk about this now. Did she acknowledge Abby's death and how it made her feel?"

"Of course not. She's been ignoring it for over twenty years, pretending everything is okay, destroying her life and my life in the process. She's so afraid of how people, like my dad, will react that she'll continue to live in her own world, no matter who gets hurt in the process."

"Like mother like son." Locky hoped the statement would hit its intended mark. He was taking a huge chance, but maybe it was the wake-up call Becket needed.

"Is that what you think I'm doing?" Becket sat up and stretched across to turn on the bedside lamp then stared down at Locky. "You do, don't you?"

"*Your* rape is your mother's Abby. If you pretend it didn't happen, you'll never be able to get on with your life, not really, because just like your mom, you'll lock yourself in a lie that will continue to haunt you."

"I've already told you, I wasn't raped. I went there looking for company with one goal in mind."

Locky pulled Becket back down and into his arms. He kissed the top of Becket's head and waited until he relaxed before continuing. "Did you ever see that old Jodie Foster movie, *The Accused*?"

"You mean that woman in the movie about that guy who was making the skin suit?"

"Yes, but that's not the movie I'm talking about. In *The Accused*, Jodie Foster played this woman who went to a college bar. She was all decked out in this really slutty outfit, dancing and getting drunk. Anyway, in the backroom of the bar, a bunch of guys gang raped her. The whole movie centres around Jodie's character trying to prove to people that she wasn't asking to be raped because of the clothes she wore or the way she acted." He tilted Becket's chin up and stared him in the eye. "Do you think if a woman wears sexy clothes it's okay for some guy to rape her?"

"Stop putting words in my mouth."

"Okay, then you tell me, did she ask to be raped?"

"Of course not, but it isn't the same. Sounds like she was awake for it, so she had to suffer through the pain and humiliation. I was asleep. At least I think I was. I don't really know for sure."

Locky held his breath. He wondered if Becket realised what he'd just admitted.

"I was raped," Becket mumbled, his voice sounding oddly...off.

"By who?" Locky asked, knowing it might be his only chance to get the truth out of Becket.

"I don't know. That's why I can't stand to think about it. I hate that I can't remember who fucked me. Just thinking about it makes me sick to my stomach."

"Where were you when it happened?"

It took so long for Becket to answer, Locky almost gave up hope. "Fallon's new place," Becket eventually said.

"Fallon's?" Locky needed to make sure.

"Yeah, but I don't think it was him. There was this other guy there that I didn't know. There was something about him..." Becket buried his face against Locky's chest. "I don't have proof, not a shred, so if you're thinking of confronting him, save your breath, I've already tried."

Locky tensed at the thought of Becket confronting the suspected rapist. "Was this other man's name Jigger?"

Becket lifted his head and met his gaze. "How do you know that?"

Locky put his hands under Becket's armpits and lifted him up his body until they were face to face. "Charlie called earlier..." he began.

* * * *

After Locky drifted off to sleep, Becket carefully eased out of bed and tip-toed into the bathroom. Like the morning after he'd been raped, he felt dirty. He grabbed a plastic sack and secured it over his cast. He'd be happy to get the damn thing off. It was a pain in the ass and then some. He turned on the shower and stepped under the spray.

The conversation had confirmed everything he'd feared, yet at the same time, part of him felt relief. It was this last feeling that made him feel dirty, because his first reaction had been elation that someone else would be the one to testify against Jigger. He was off the hook, so why didn't he feel better about it?

"Is this a private party?" Locky asked.

One thing was certain in Becket's mind. Despite everything else going on, Locky was still the best thing to ever come into his life. He opened the shower curtain to find a gloriously nude hunk of a man waiting on the other side. "Only if you've come prepared."

Locky's dark eyebrows shot up in surprise. He held up his finger. "Give me a minute."

Becket laughed as Locky sprinted out of the bathroom. While he was gone, Becket picked up the soap and began to thoroughly clean his dick and ass. He hadn't planned on having sex with Locky for the first time in the shower, but the time seemed right and damn it, Becket wasn't about to let the moment pass him by because of a little thing like location.

Locky returned to the bathroom with the supplies, but Becket noticed a difference in Locky's expression. "You're not going to back out on me again, are you?" Becket asked.

"I need to ask you something, well, actually, I need you to promise me something." Locky set the lube and condoms on the side of the tub and waited.

"Okay," Becket agreed. It was obvious Locky had something serious on his mind, and for some reason the divide between them felt like more than just a five-inch slab of porcelain. He turned off the water and grabbed a towel off the rack. "What is it?"

Locky followed Becket's lead and wrapped a towel around his waist. "You're young," he began.

Becket held up his hands. "Please don't start this again. I thought we were beyond it."

"We are — that's not what I'm worried about."

"Then what?" Instead of standing in the cold bathroom, Becket swiped the lube and condoms off the side of the tub and walked into the bedroom. He set the supplies on the bedside table along with the wet plastic sack, before dropping his towel and climbing in bed. It still wasn't clear whether or not

Locky planned to kibosh the whole thing, but it sure as hell wouldn't be because Becket didn't want it.

"For the first time in your life you're free to do what you want, when you want."

"Yeah and right now I want you." Becket thought he'd already made that clear.

Locky sat on the opposite queen bed and faced Becket. "I know you do, and Lord help me, I want you, too. But in the last few days, one of my biggest fears has resurfaced and I'm worried."

Becket's entire focus was on the first half of Locky's statement, so it took him several moments for the second half to catch up. "Wait, why would you be afraid of me?"

"Not you, the way I feel about you. I already care a great deal, and I know I'm only going to fall deeper the more time I spend with you."

"So what's the problem?"

"You're not ready for what I want, and there's no way in hell I'd expect you to be, not now, not after everything you've been through." Locky stood and moved to kneel beside Becket's bed. "You're gonna break my heart, and I know it, but damn it, I want you anyway."

Becket peeled back the covers and welcomed Locky under them. "I may just surprise you."

Locky tore off his towel and joined Becket. "Light on or off?"

Becket paused at the question. Although he'd spent the previous school year making up for his lack of sex growing up in Crescent Ridge, he'd never had an actual boyfriend. Most of his encounters happened in the occasional dorm room, bar bathroom or parked car. He was ashamed to admit he didn't really know what was expected. "Umm, I don't know. Whatever you want is fine."

Locky got out of bed and walked to the window. He opened the heavy drapes to the setting sunlight. "We'll compromise." He slid back in bed and turned off the lamp. Bathed in a soft orange hue, the room felt warm, safe.

Becket rested his head against Locky's chest. He felt oddly uneasy, and wasn't ashamed to admit it. "I'm nervous."

Locky wrapped his arms around Becket and rolled them both until they were face to face on their sides. "Don't be. You've been through a traumatic event. If you decide all you want to do is lay in my arms all night, I'm okay with that. It's whatever you're comfortable with."

Becket grinned. Bless Locky and his sensitive heart. "I'm not nervous because of what happened to me." He traced Locky's eyebrows with his fingertips. "This is special, and I've never had something special."

Locky started with a soft kiss, slowly working into a deeper, more passionate play of tongues. Becket returned each touch and moan and soon forgot all about being nervous. He gave himself over to Locky's tender handling and immediately noticed the difference. His usual hook-up involved rough groping, sloppy kisses with little to no thought or feeling behind them and either a blowjob or a quick fuck.

Locky took his time in demonstrating his skills as a lover. No wonder the man was so confident in his abilities. Within minutes, Becket was putty in Locky's hands. He put up no resistance when Locky pushed down the covers and began to explore Becket's body with his mouth and hands.

Becket tucked his casted hand under Locky's abandoned pillow, hoping it would be enough to remind him of the heavy plaster and the damage it could inflict if his passion got out of control. Spreadeagle on the bed, Becket watched as Locky neared his cock. It wasn't safe, not completely, not yet. He reached down and threaded his fingers through Locky's thick dark hair. "You probably shouldn't do that without a condom."

Locky looked up at Becket with a wicked grin. "Oh, don't worry about that, I'm not going to let you come yet. I'm going to tease you until you're out of your mind."

"Really? I'm twenty. I can come with no other help than a stiff breeze and a billboard of a hot guy," Becket countered.

Laughing, Locky tickled Becket's balls with the tip of his tongue.

"I wasn't kidding," Becket warned.

Locky encircled the base of Becket's cock with his fingers and squeezed with enough pressure to prolong Becket's pleasure. "Will that help?"

Becket had never worn a cock ring, but he was beginning to understand their worth. "Hope so."

Locky resumed his attention to Becket's balls, laving and sucking them into the warmth of his mouth. *Holy fuck.* Even with the pressure on his cock, Becket had to bite the inside of his cheek to keep from shooting.

"I don't think I can do this," Becket admitted.

Locky immediately pulled back and sat up. "I'm sorry. I didn't mean to make you uncomfortable, I was just…"

"Shut up," Becket interrupted. "I meant I can't *not* come when you're doing that."

With a relieved sigh, Locky fell back to the bed and moved up to rest his head beside Becket's. "Maybe it would be better to stick to the basics for now."

"Do the basics still involve you fucking me?" Becket asked.

"Most definitely." Locky leaned in and gave Becket another round of deep kisses before reaching for the supplies on the bedside table. "You're a good kisser."

Becket shrugged in mock-arrogance. "You're not the only one who's picked up skills along the way."

Locky poured lube onto his fingers and reached between Becket's spread legs. "Show me more of those skills."

Becket initiated another kiss just as Locky's slick finger began to stretch his hole. While Becket prided himself on his kissing and blowjob skills, it seemed Locky's expertise were never ending. The gentle slide of Locky's finger was yet another reminder that Becket was finally with someone who cared.

Becket reached down and wrapped his hand around Locky's cock. Even more magnificent than Becket had ever imagined, Locky's cock was a road map of thick veins. There was no question in Becket's mind how good the ridged dick would feel fucking in and out of him.

Locky pushed another finger inside Becket's hole. "Okay?"

"I'd rather have something bigger." Becket squeezed Locky's cock to punctuate his point.

Locky ignored Becket's plea and continued to stretch him using his fingers. It wasn't until he'd worked up to three moving easily in and out of Becket's ass that he reached for the condom. He fumbled with the foil package for several moments before eventually handing it to Becket. "My hand's too slippery."

Becket took the condom without mentioning the visible shaking of Locky's hands. He easily opened the foil wrapper and held it up. Could it be that Locky was as excited as he was, or was it a case of nerves that kept Locky from his task? Becket smiled to himself in satisfaction. It didn't really matter why Locky's hands shook, it was reassuring to know he wasn't the only one affected.

"Thanks," Locky mumbled, rolling the condom down his length.

"I'm here to please." Although Becket said it in a teasing manner, the words were sincere.

Locky rolled on top of Becket and insinuated himself between Becket's spread thighs. At the first touch of Locky's cock against his hole, Becket sent a silent thank you to the man upstairs. He wrapped his legs around Locky and urged him in.

Staring down at him, Locky's jaw muscles began to tighten and twitch as he eased his way inside. "So good," he ground out.

"Mmm hmm." Becket was beyond speech at the moment. He was lost in a world that centred around the fat cock of his dreams rocking its way as deep into his ass as it would go. It was a glorious world, one he hoped to return to again and again.

Buried to the root, Locky hissed out a breath. "Fuck." He gave Becket a few heartbeats to get used to the size of his cock before he started to move.

Becket closed his eyes and tried to relax, making it easier for Locky. Ideas began racing through his mind of all the places in BK they could sneak away to fuck. Locky had made it clear to Becket the previous year that he didn't get involved with residents. Becket wondered if that was a house rule or a personal one.

Locky's thrusts increased in speed and intensity, bringing Becket out of his daydream. He opened his eyes and propped himself up enough to see the joining of Locky's body with his. Sexy didn't begin to describe the way Locky's dick looked sliding in and out of Becket's hole. Becket reached for his cock and began stroking himself, paying particular attention to the underside of his crown.

Becket's stomach muscles began to tighten as his breathing picked up, a sure sign that he was moments away from climax. "Close," he managed to say between pants.

Locky nodded his head, whether in permission or agreement, Becket didn't know but he'd take it regardless. He aimed his cock towards his own stomach and shot a thick load of pearly white cum onto his abdomen, one drop landing high on his chest. "Fuuuck!"

By the time the last strand left his cock, Becket worried that he'd forgotten how to breathe. He searched desperately for each indrawn breath of air, hoping he wouldn't pass out and make a fool of himself.

Locky landed on top of Becket, making the fight for oxygen even more difficult. Becket pushed at Locky's chest for several seconds before Locky was able to roll himself to Becket's side.

Bathed in the last light of the setting sun, Becket and Locky lay side by side, each of them fighting to slow their heart rate. Finally, Becket licked his lips and turned his head to stare at Locky. "I thought I was going to either pass out or die."

It took Locky a moment to answer. "Yeah."

With his energy drained, Becket was barely able to reach to the floor to grab his bath towel. He did his best to clean his cum from Locky's stomach and his own before collapsing again. "I wonder if Mom's planning to sleep here."

"I thought you wanted to take her back to the farm tonight." Locky gathered Becket in his arms and kissed his forehead.

"I'm too exhausted to make the drive tonight. Besides, I think I need to try to talk to her again. I don't know, maybe I should talk to Dad instead."

It sucked. Physically Becket was on cloud nine, but mentally he was still confused as to how to handle his mom. In his heart, he knew he would have to eventually walk away if his mom didn't agree to go for help. The last few minutes had proven to him that his future and a chance with Locky meant too much for him to give up.

"Whatever you decide, I think you owe it to your brothers to tell them the truth."

Becket gave Locky a gentle kiss. "No matter what happens, I'm gonna be sitting beside you on that plane when the time comes."

"That's all I needed to hear," Locky replied.

Chapter Six

The ringing of his phone woke Locky from a sound sleep. He turned on the light and searched the floor until he came up with his jeans, eventually finding the cell in his pocket long after it had stopped ringing.

"Becket?" he called out, wondering why he'd been in bed alone. He spotted a note on the bedside table and smiled.

"Going to the hospital. Come on over when you wake up, and I'll buy you breakfast. Love, B." Locky crawled back into bed and read the note twice more. He knew it was just a quick message, but the closing made him feel...content, something he hadn't felt in...ever, he realised.

After setting the paper on the table, Locky opened his phone and checked his message.

"Hey, it's Jack," the voicemail began. "Charlie's convinced that that Jigger fellow did something to hurt Becket. Give us a call back as soon as you can."

Locky felt uneasy about sharing Becket's secret, but Charlie was in charge of BK House and had a right to know. He settled a pillow against the headboard and leant back while he waited for Jack to answer.

"Did I wake you?" Jack asked.

"Yeah. Long night." Locky didn't dare tell Jack he'd spent it fucking Becket between short naps.

"Is Becket there?"

"No, he's at the hospital. I think his dad might get out sometime today." Locky still didn't know if Becket would follow his parents to the farm or if they'd fly home together.

"Did you listen to my message?" Jack asked.

"I did, and yeah it happened. Becket can't confirm it was Jigger who drugged him, but the only three people at the bar that night were Becket, Jigger and Fallon. Believe me, I plan to have a long talk with Fallon about leaving Becket alone with a guy like that."

"I don't think Fallon knew about Jigger's past. He's sunk a hell of a lot of money into that place, I can't see him hiring an ex-con on purpose."

"He's an ex-con?" Locky sat up and swung his legs over the side of the bed. His blood was boiling. "What the fuck is wrong with Fallon? Didn't he do background checks? Sounds to me like he knows nothing about running a bar."

"He doesn't, but that's beside the point. What're we going to do about Becket?" Jack's concern was obvious in his softer tone.

"He still has a few things here to deal with, but once we're outta here, I'll try and get him to talk to the police. He'll resist, I've no doubt about that, but it'll be the best thing for him. I think he still feels guilty because he went to Fallon's with hopes of getting laid." Just saying it aloud was enough to raise Locky's blood pressure. After the night they'd spent together, he didn't like the thought of Becket trolling the bars for action.

"I'm sure Charlie'll want to talk to you about what we can do once you get back."

"Do me a favour and ask him if we can keep this between us for now. I don't know whether or not we'll get Becket to talk to the police, but I'm fairly sure he wouldn't want the other guys in the house to know, at least not until he's ready to tell them."

"I hear what you're saying. The only one we might have trouble with is Chase. He's bugged Charlie a couple times a day, asking if anyone's heard from Becket. I think he's worried."

"I think Becket needs to deal with it. Just tell Chase that we'll be back by Friday at the latest." Locky stood and headed for the bathroom.

"Will do. Call if you need anything."

"Sure thing." Locky hung up and set the phone on the counter beside the sink. If he didn't get his ass in gear and get to the hospital, Becket would be buying him lunch instead of breakfast.

* * * *

Becket chose a table behind a large potted plant and set his tray down. He'd left the hotel room that morning without getting a kiss and he was dying for one.

"It's like a jungle back here," Locky commented as he joined Becket.

"It's all about the privacy." Becket leaned over and kissed Locky. "I wish I could've stayed in bed with you this morning, but I wanted to talk to Mom. Sooo I called her and she met me here." Becket pointed to the other side of the cafeteria. "Well, there, actually, but you get the idea."

Locky chuckled before taking a drink of his cranberry juice. "So where'd she stay last night?"

"On one of the couches in the waiting room." Becket didn't tell Locky that his mom refused to sleep at the hotel because he was there. She still blamed Locky for what she considered Becket's betrayal, and no amount of talking would change her mind. "Dad's being released as soon as the doctor signs him out, so they'll all be heading home later today."

"They? Does that mean we're flying back?"

"She told me to." Actually, she told Becket that Locky wasn't allowed to step foot in her house, but Locky didn't need to know that. "She's still refusing to see a doctor."

"Do you know what you're going to do?"

Becket shrugged, he'd thought of nothing else since the talk with his mom. "What *can* I do? She just keeps telling me that she thought I was on her side, and now that she knows the truth, I should just go back to school."

"You have to tell either one of your brothers or your dad. You can't leave without letting someone know."

"Why? I've spent two years away from home and nothing's happened. Except for yesterday, her lapses have always been nothing more than believing Abby's still alive." Truth be told, Becket needed a break after their morning meeting. It hurt that his mom refused to see Locky for the kind man he really was.

"I think it's time you told your dad. The situation's not like it was back then, it's just the two of them. Maybe he'll be able to spend more time with her now."

It was obvious to Becket that Locky still didn't understand their family dynamic. "Do you know how many times I've spoken to my dad since I've been here? Zero. I ducked into the room once, but he was asleep. *But*, here's the funny part, he knows I'm here yet he's never asked about me. I know it's weird, but it's normal. There's no way I can walk into his room and tell him that I've helped mom hide her illness all these years." Becket shook his head. "I can't do it."

"So talk to Cade. He's still here, right?" Locky went back to eating his breakfast.

"Yeah, he's here." Becket knew Cade already suspected that what had happened in the elevator wasn't an isolated incident, so if he handed the torch off to anyone it would be him. "He'll hate me if I saddle him with Mom's secret."

Locky ran his fingers through his hair, looking completely exasperated. "I don't know what to tell you, except you have your own things to deal with, and I don't think you can do that and worry about Carrie at the same time."

"I'll always worry about her, she's my mom. Don't you ever worry about your mom?"

Locky gathered his uneaten food onto the tray. "My mom's a genuine, old school, born into money bitch. Believe me, she can take care of herself."

Becket had never heard someone talk about his or her mother that way. The words stung, but the emotion behind them was obvious. "I'm sorry."

"Thanks. I was too for the first ten years of my life, but then she sent me off to boarding school, and I realised I was a better person without her." Locky laughed, but it didn't sound very jovial. "I usually went to friends' houses during breaks. That's where I learned what normal was."

Becket's heart broke. He'd been so wrapped up in his own crap, that he hadn't even taken the time to ask about Locky's family. "I suck."

Locky let out a genuine chuckle. "Yes, you do, and very well, I might add."

"No, I mean it. I should've asked about your mom and dad. I'm not a very good boyfriend." *Shit.* Becket winced. "Not that I'm your boyfriend or anything."

"I'd love for you to be my boyfriend, but I don't want to tie you down with that term." Locky gave Becket a quick kiss. "Let's just say we enjoy spending time together. If, in another year or so, you still feel the same way, we can put a label on it."

"But I like that label," Becket mumbled.

"Me, too. So let's move forward with that in mind." Locky stood and stretched his arms over his head. "I hate to bring it up, but if you're going to talk to Cade, you should probably do it. If you want, I can call the airline and see if we can fly out a day early?"

Becket got to his feet. "Yeah, I guess I need to get back and deal with stuff there. I'm like a fucked up version of Johnny Appleseed, only I sprinkle trouble wherever I go."

Despite their very public location, Locky pulled Becket into his arms. "You're not sprinkling trouble. You're trying to fight your way out of a forest that someone else planted."

"Yeah, well, I'd better sharpen my axe and get upstairs before Dad checks out."

Locky kissed Becket, heedless of who might be around. "I'll go back to the hotel and get our stuff packed."

Becket nodded. It was hard to believe he'd only been in Iowa for three days. How was it possible that his life could change so much, for the good and bad, in that short amount of time? "Walk me to the elevator?"

"You bet."

* * * *

Becket found Cade sitting alone in the waiting room. "Where's Mom and Julie?"

Cade glanced up from his book. "Mom's in with Dad getting his discharge instructions, and Julie's shopping. She said she couldn't leave Des Moines without visiting a few of her favourite stores."

Becket settled into a chair, leaving an empty space between the two of them. "I need to talk to you about Mom."

"I'm not taking sides. I know she's upset because you brought your...boyfriend here, but what did you expect? Mom and Dad have always been tolerant with the way you are, but that doesn't mean it's fair of you to shove it in their faces."

Becket waved his hands to stop Cade from continuing. "That's not why she's mad. She may have told you that, but that's not the reason."

"Then what is?" Cade set down his book and leant down to rest his forearms on his thighs.

"I told her that I'd help her find a doctor before I went back to school. I thi..."

"She's sick?" Cade asked, cutting Becket off.

"No. I mean, I think she's in pretty good health physically." Becket went on to explain his mom's lapses and how he'd dealt with them and helped her hide them from the rest of the family throughout the years.

By the time Becket finished, Cade had gone pale. "Are you okay?"

Cade scrubbed his hands over his face and shook his head. "No, I'm pissed."

Becket thought of getting up and running for his life. Cade was one of those gentle giants until he got angry. Becket hadn't witnessed Cade's temper often, but someone usually got hurt the few times he did. "I'm sorry. I wanted to tell you years ago, but Mom said you'd go to Dad and he'd put her back into the hospital. She said I was the only one she could trust to keep her secret."

Cade finally sat up. His complexion had gone from white to red. "I'm not mad at you. How can I be? You were just a kid when she started manipulating you." He stood and started to pace back and forth. "I was seventeen. I should've known better."

"What're you talking about, you knew?" Becket couldn't believe what he was hearing.

"No, I didn't, which doesn't make me son of the year. I'm talking about Dad. It seems they're both master manipulators. To make matters even worse, I think Dad's known all along that Mom's still sick."

"No, he doesn't. Mom's terrified of him finding out," Becket argued.

Cade sat in the chair next to Becket. "Dad caught Scotty and me in the barn fooling around when I was seventeen. He ran Scotty off, and then he sat me down and told me Mom wouldn't be able to handle it if she knew what I'd been doing with my best friend. He said she'd never fully recovered from Abby's death and something like that would push her over the edge. Said if I really loved her, I would spare her that."

Becket's heart skipped a beat at the announcement. How could he not have known his brother was gay? It said a lot about their relationship. For the first time since he came out, he understood why Cade had avoided him after hearing the news. "That's why you hated me, isn't it?"

Cade nodded. "You were always Mom's favourite, which had been hard enough to handle, but when you came out and she seemed to support you, it drove the point home that you could do no wrong in her eyes. So, yeah, I hated you. By then I was married to Julie and Dad's heart was already giving him problems." He looked at Becket. "I felt trapped and there was nothing I could do about it."

It was a lot to take in. Becket leant back in his chair and rested his head against the wall behind him. "So what now?"

"I don't know. Maybe it's time we let our parents act like the adults they're supposed to be. I know one thing, I'm gonna take Scotty up on his offer to help work his farm." Cade's hand landed on Becket's thigh and gave it a reassuring squeeze. "And you're going to go back to Idaho and finish what you started."

"What about Mom? Do you think she'll be okay?"

"You still don't get it, do you? It would be different if she had her lapses and didn't remember them, didn't talk about them, but that's not the case. She knew exactly what she was doing when she brainwashed you into lying for her. Abby died twenty-three years ago. If Mom wanted to get better, she would've done something about it before now. The fact that she's angry with you because you suggested she get help only proves it. Maybe she likes visiting with Abby from time to time, or maybe, and this is what I'd put my money on, she likes being the victim. Mom wants you to feel sorry for her. She wants you to feel guilty every time you leave her because it gives her control over you."

The bitterness radiating off Cade was almost suffocating. For years, Becket had felt sorry for himself because he'd had to carry the burden of his mom's secret alone, but at least he'd been allowed to leave. Cade had never felt he had that option. Yeah, if Becket were in Cade's shoes, he would probably be just as bitter, if not more so. "Locky's making arrangements. We're flying out sometime today."

"Good. I could've never said this before today, but you deserve it. Just do me a favour."

"Sure," Becket agreed.

"For the next while, don't answer Mom's phone calls. I have a feeling things might get worse before they can get better, but if she wants to be in her children's lives, she needs to take the first step on her own."

"What about Nic and Del?" It would be hard for Becket to resist the urge to check on his mom, but he'd follow Cade's advice.

"I'll talk to them once we get Dad settled. I'll continue to work the farm as long as Del and Nic need my help, but I'm going to let them know I'd rather be elsewhere."

"I'm proud of you," Becket couldn't resist saying. "I can't imagine what you've been through, but I want only the best for you from here on."

Cade stood and pulled Becket into a hug. As far as Becket could remember, it was the first hug he'd received from his big brother since he was a kid. Becket wrapped his arms around Cade, being careful not to clunk him in the head with his cast, and hugged him back. "I love you, brother," Cade whispered in Becket's ear.

"I love you, too, and I hope maybe we can become friends someday." Becket had always wondered what it would be like to have a close relationship with his brothers, and with a little work and hope, he was starting to believe he might get his wish.

Cade released him and took a step back. "Careful what you wish for. By the time the dust settles, you may be the only family member who'll have anything to do with me."

"You're wrong. Mom and Dad might have their issues, but Del and Nic have always looked up to you. Just like I have," Becket added.

Cade looked uneasy. "Sorry I acted the way I did. I was angry that you had the guts to stand up for yourself, something I obviously couldn't do."

Their mom walked into the waiting room, putting an end to Becket and Cade's bonding moment. He looked at her, hoping she'd say something nice after their morning argument, but she turned her gaze away from him and spoke to Cade.

"Your dad's ready. Would you pull the truck up front?"

"Sure." Cade gave Becket another hug. "Call me?"

"Absolutely."

* * * *

Locky pulled out of the airport parking lot and headed home, back to BK House. Becket had filled him in on his conversation with Cade, and Locky couldn't have been more surprised. He was usually good at picking gay men out of a crowd, but he would have never guessed Cade preferred men over women.

Becket turned sideways in the seat and stared at Locky. "I guess this is the point when we're supposed to talk about how things are gonna work between us once we get back."

Locky reached over and brushed the back of his hand across Becket's cheek. "Good question."

"Will you get in trouble if Charlie finds out?"

"I have a feeling he already knows I care about you, but I'm not sure how he'll react once he discovers we're sleeping together." He sighed. "When I started at BK, he told me I wasn't allowed to get sexually involved with the students."

"So should we sneak around? I don't mind if it means saving your job."

Locky had spent the last year of his life trying to hide his attraction to Becket. After finally giving in to his feelings, he doubted he'd be able to fool anyone, especially Charlie. "No, no sneaking. Guess I'll have to talk to Charlie."

"Does that mean I can sleep with you tonight?"

"I don't even know if I'll have a place to live by tonight. Why don't we wait and see what happens." The threat of losing his job wasn't enough to keep him from the man he wanted. Even thinking about it caused a niggle in the back of his mind. What if he gave up everything and Becket outgrew him in a few months?

Becket leaned his seat back. "This car's pretty comfortable. I can sleep in here with you if it comes to that."

Locky smiled, reassured that he was doing the right thing, knowing each day that he spent with Becket was a gift. "Good to know."

* * * *

When they arrived at the house, Becket took his suitcase upstairs and Locky went in search of Charlie.

He found him in the kitchen, perched on a stool at the island while Jack prepared dinner. "We're back."

"Is Becket with you?" Charlie asked, turning his body to face Locky.

"Yeah, he's upstairs." Locky opened the refrigerator and removed a bottle of water. "Any news on Jigger?"

"No, but Fallon stopped by earlier looking for Becket. I think he's figured out why Becket's been avoiding him."

"Did you tell Fallon to stay away from him?" Locky asked before draining the water bottle.

"No, I didn't. That's something Becket needs to decide for himself," Charlie countered.

"How can you be so nonchalant about it? Fallon's the one who put Becket in danger in the first place."

"I disagree. Becket's the one who went to the bar. Fallon's no more guilty than Becket," Charlie argued.

"That's what I figured you'd say," Becket said, stepping into the kitchen. "That's why I didn't want anyone to know."

Locky could've strangled Charlie. Although he knew what Charlie meant by the comment, it was clear Becket didn't. "That's not what he meant."

"No, it isn't," Charlie was quick to say. He climbed off the stool and walked towards Becket.

"That's not what it sounded like to me." Becket turned and left the room before Charlie could reach him.

"Shit." Locky tossed his bottle into the recycle bin. "I thought I finally had him convinced that it wasn't his fault."

"It isn't. That's not what I was trying to say." Charlie turned to Jack. "Is that what I said?"

Jack, who had kept out of the conversation thus far, set his spoon down. "No, that's not what you said, but

I can see how Becket would've interpreted it, if that's the way he already felt." He turned his attention to Locky. "Go after him. If he's going to listen to anyone it'll be you."

There was something about the way Jack said it that led Locky to believe his feelings for Becket had already been made quite clear. "Answer me one thing before I leave. Am I going to be fired?"

"No," Charlie answered. "We have a few things to talk about, but now's not the time."

"Thanks." Locky started out of the room. "I'll go find him."

"See if you can talk him into going to the police," Jack said.

"Yeah." After Becket's reaction to Charlie's statement, Locky wasn't sure he'd ever be able to convince Becket to admit to the authorities what had happened to him.

* * * *

"I've been looking everywhere for you," Locky said, entering the small meditation garden at the back of the property.

Becket had picked at his cast until the plaster was starting to crumble around his hand. It was almost ready to come off anyway. "I needed to think."

Locky sat on the bench beside Becket. "I know Charlie hurt your feelings, but he honestly didn't mean what you thought he did. He was mad at me for being angry with Fallon. Charlie was trying to make me understand that both of you are innocent in all this, that the only one to blame is Jigger."

"I don't want to testify. I can't sit in front of that man, and not know what all he did to me." Becket abandoned the destruction of his cast. He rested his head on Locky's shoulder, needing the strength Locky always seemed to possess. "What if Jigger says I begged him to fuck me? I watched him every night before I came here, and I've seen him leave Fallon's place with a dozen different guys, men who obviously went with him willingly."

"You didn't tell me you'd been watching him every night." Locky wrapped an arm around Becket. "The thought of you taking that chance scares the shit out of me."

"I couldn't bring myself to tell anyone, but that doesn't mean I didn't worry about other people."

"Which is why you need to go to the police. I would imagine Jigger's other victim is scared, too. Don't you think it would help him to know he doesn't have to stand alone? Besides, the more charges that are piled on Jigger, the more likely he is to get sent away for a very long time. That's what you want, right?"

Damn Locky for making sense. "Would you go with me?"

"To the police station? Absolutely."

Closing his eyes, Becket burrowed further against Locky's side. He wondered if Jigger's other victim had someone as kind and gentle to lean on. "Tomorrow," he finally said.

Chapter Seven

"I don't understand. You're saying that my rape doesn't count?" Becket asked the prosecuting attorney.

"Of course that's not what I'm saying. It's a matter of what we can make stick, and I'm sorry, Mr Chandler, but we have no physical evidence that Paul Williams raped you. The best we could hope for would be to find some of the drug in one of your hair follicles, but not even that will prove Paul Williams slipped it in your drink. If I put you on the stand, there's a chance that your testimony will simply muddy the water. We have a pretty solid case against Mr Williams on the evidence and testimony gathered from Mr Kloiber. I know it's not easy to hear, and I do apologise."

Becket stood. "Have a nice life," he told the balding man.

He'd endured countless hours of embarrassing questions by the detective in charge of the case and the prosecutor's office over the last few months, and now that they were ready for trial, he'd learnt it had been all for nothing. To say he was furious would be an understatement. Why had they made him go through all that if they weren't going to do anything with the fucking information he provided? Did they think it was easy for him to relive the biggest shame of his life over and over for perfect strangers?

The only good thing to come out of the entire ordeal was the new friendship he'd forged with Eric Kloiber. Unlike Becket, Eric hadn't 'officially' been out of the closet when he was raped, which made it even harder on him. Becket wondered how Eric would react when he discovered he'd be the prosecutor's star witness.

Becket left the courthouse and found Locky sitting on a bench in the shade. "Let's go."

Locky looked up from his phone and frowned. "Something wrong?"

"They don't want me. I 'muddy the water' of their case because evidently I'm not believable enough to get past the no evidence thing. Bastards."

"That's bullshit." Locky stood and reached for Becket's hand. "I'm sorry. I wish I knew what to say."

"You can go back in there and stick your foot up that dickhead's ass. Barring that, you can kiss me and tell me you're proud of me for even talking to them in the first place." He tilted his chin up and waited for the medicine that would make him feel better. Predictably, he received a double dose and an invitation to lunch. *Score.*

* * * *

The alarm woke Locky on the day of Jigger's trial. He rolled to his back and reached over to slap the snooze button.

"I don't want it to be morning yet," Becket grumbled and covered his head with a pillow.

Locky grabbed the pillow and tossed it to the foot of the bed before pulling Becket into his arms. Despite the very real possibility that they both had bad breath, Locky leaned in and proceeded to kiss Becket awake.

The trial couldn't have come at a worse time for Becket. He was in the middle of midterms and trying to study while keeping close tabs on his new friend, and fellow victim, Eric. Lately, it seemed Becket was either studying in class or trying to keep Eric's mind off the upcoming trial, but Locky never made an issue of it.

Locky moved to insinuate himself between Becket's legs, putting their morning woods in direct contact. He missed Becket like crazy when he wasn't around, but he knew being busy was a normal routine for college students.

Breaking the kiss, Locky reached for the bottle of lube on the bedside table. "Do we have time for this before your class?"

Becket glanced at the clock. "As long as I'm in the shower by seven-thirty, I can make it."

"We'll make it quick then," Locky turned off the alarm before pouring lube onto his fingers.

"Not too quick." Becket kissed Locky's chin. "I've missed you. Sorry I got in so late. Eric had had his last meeting with the dickhead prosecutor the day before, so he was pretty wigged."

Locky ran a slicked finger around the pucker of Becket's hole several times before pushing inside. Part of Locky still felt guilty for convincing Becket to go to the police in the first place, but he knew it was a big step in him taking back his life.

After several months of sleeping together, it didn't take long for Locky to prepare Becket. He took the unwrapped condom from Becket and grinned. Since their first time, Becket always made it a point to open the foil packet, and as usual, Locky was grateful. "I don't understand why they can't make those easier to open," he grumbled as he rolled it down his length.

"Because it gives people a little more time to back out of those one night stands. Not everyone has a fantastically helpful boyfriend to do it for them," Becket said, draping his legs over Locky's shoulders.

"You are a fantastically helpful boyfriend, but I've got exactly twelve minutes to have my wicked way with you before you have to get in the shower." Locky guided the head of his cock to Becket's hole and eased his way inside. His eyes drifted closed as he leant down for a deep kiss. It was his favourite way to fuck, his cock buried to the hilt while his tongue duelled with Becket's.

Becket reached between them and tickled Locky's cock with his fingertips as it slid in and out of his hole. "Love this. Love to feel you," Becket whispered.

The four letter word had been used often between them lately, but neither had professed their love for each other. Locky knew it was fear that kept him from telling Becket how much he cared. His mother had told him once when he was a child that his love was smothering. Now grown, he knew she'd said it because she didn't know the first thing about giving or receiving affection, but the words continued to haunt him, cursing him in some way.

Staring into Becket's big brown eyes, Locky continued to fuck him with everything he had, while his heart silently begged to be loved in return. Becket still had a little over a year and a half of school left, more if he decided to go for his Masters. Locky continued to tell himself that he wouldn't try to tie Becket down until he'd experienced everything college life had to offer. It wasn't easy, as a matter of fact, it was a daily fight to keep his emotions in check around Becket, but he thought he'd done a pretty good job.

"Yeah. Oh, fuck, yeah, just like that," Becket babbled, his voice growing louder and louder.

Locky kissed Becket again in an effort to keep the evidence of their lovemaking from every other resident of BK. When Becket cried out his climax, even Locky's deep kiss wasn't enough to muffle the sound. He was all for enthusiasm, but part of his bargain with Charlie was to keep the sexual relationship low-key while in the house, no groping or kissing in public rooms and no screaming like banshees while having sex.

Becket broke away from Locky's kiss and gasped. "Shit, you're trying to kill me."

Locky slammed into Becket, hard. He still had a few more minutes to fuck and he wasn't going to stop until he had to. "We're gonna have to get you a muffle."

Becket reached for Locky's balls. "Yeah, let's see how quiet you can be," he challenged.

Crying out wasn't something Locky usually had a problem with. It wasn't that the sex wasn't blow-your-head-off fantastic, but his throat generally seized up along with the rest of his body when he came.

The added stimulus of Becket's fondling broke Locky's concentration and before he could stop the runaway train, he climaxed. It took a great deal of willpower not to cry out Becket's name, but Locky managed to trap it all into a low, deep growl as he shot load after load into the condom.

Becket removed his legs from Locky's shoulders and pulled him down against him. "You won this round, warrior, but I demand a rematch."

With a gasping laugh, Locky buried his face between the curve of Becket's shoulder and neck. "Tonight, same place, less talk."

At the last possible moment before Becket had to jump in the shower, Locky rolled off and removed the condom. "I'll pick you up in front of the Biology Lab at eleven-thirty. I thought we could grab some lunch before heading to the courthouse."

Groaning, Becket slowly sat up and climbed off the bed. "Sounds good." He found his underwear and pulled them on along with his sweat pants. "You think Charlie would mind if Eric slept in my room for a while?"

Locky's heart nearly stopped at the question. He'd always made it clear to Becket that he wouldn't stand in the way if Becket wanted to see other people, but right under his nose? The thought that he could be so easily replaced in Becket's bed was even more heartbreaking than he'd imagined. "You'll have to ask him," Locky mumbled. "I guess I didn't realise things between the two of you were headed in that direction."

Clutching his T-shirt and sneakers, Becket stopped on his way to the door and turned back to stare at Locky. "I don't know what the fuck you have in your head, but Eric's been having trouble in the dorm. I thought since I've been sleeping up here every night, that it would be okay for him to crash in my bed."

Without warning, Becket reared back and threw one of his shoes at Locky. "You asshole. Why would you think I wanted to sleep with someone else?"

Locky blocked the shoe with his forearm. "Sorry. I misunderstood." He wrapped the used condom in a tissue and tossed it into the trashcan before getting out of bed. Shoe in hand, he walked over to Becket. Holding out the impromptu weapon, he knew he'd fucked up. "I'll talk to Charlie about Eric if you'll forgive me?"

Becket took his shoe back and shook it at Locky. "We need to talk. Lucky for you, I have a chem test in thirty minutes." He gave Locky a quick kiss. "Eleven-thirty," he said before walking out of the room.

Frustrated with himself, Locky ran his fingers through his hair. He knew if he didn't get his jealousy under control he'd lose the one thing he cherished more than anything else in the world, Becket.

His phone rang, interrupting his self-berating. He snagged the phone off the table. "Hello."

"Hey," Cade greeted. "How's he doing?"

Since leaving Iowa, Locky and Becket had kept in close contact with Cade. After Becket had finally shared what had happened to him with his oldest brother, Cade had become even more diligent about checking in on the baby of the family. "Hard to say. He's been keeping himself busy with school, but I know today is going to be tough on him."

"That's what I figured, so Del, Nic and I decided to fly up to support him. We're at the Sunset Motel off the highway."

Locky was stunned by the announcement. "You're here?"

"Yeah. It's the first time the three of us have taken a trip together without the wives, so we went out to that club Becket told us about."

"Fallon's?" It was hard to believe the Chandler brothers would visit the place where their brother may or may not have been raped. "Why?"

"I don't know. Seemed like a good idea at the time. I think Nic and Del wanted to lean on the owner about what really happened in his bar, but the guy wasn't there and the bouncer was like a rabid bulldog when we asked about him."

Locky had never liked Fallon, but he'd come to realise that, other than being neglectful in checking out his employees, he'd done nothing wrong. "It's probably a good thing he wasn't there. That bouncer you spoke to is a highly paid bodyguard Fallon hired to protect him from all the wackos and media that have been coming around."

"There're three of us, we could've handled ourselves. Regardless, we stayed and got shit-faced. Del and Nic are still sleeping it off, but I thought I'd check in with you to see what time you both were heading to the courthouse."

"Becket has a big test this morning, so we decided to wait and go to the afternoon session. Becket's friend won't take the stand until sometime late today." Locky still couldn't get over the fact that the Chandler brothers had flown in. "Becket's going to be shocked that you're here. I'm picking him up at eleven-thirty. I thought I'd take him to La Cocina for lunch, it's just down from the courthouse on the square."

"Would you mind if we joined you?" Cade asked.

"Not at all, Becket'll be thrilled to see you."

"Hope so. See ya there."

Cade hung up, and Locky was left scratching his head. He wondered who was taking care of the farm with all three brothers gone. Surely Becket's dad,

James, wasn't well enough to take on the task by himself.

Locky headed for the bathroom. It wasn't his place to worry about the farm. He had Becket and a houseful of students to take care of.

* * * *

By the time they reached the Mexican restaurant, Becket's lips were red and swollen. He assumed his need for Locky's perfect mouth on his had something to do with his nerves, regardless, Locky had indulged him at every stop light on the way.

Locky turned off the engine and leaned over for another deep kiss. "I guess this means you're not mad anymore."

"I wouldn't say mad was ever the right word, hurt maybe." Actually, hurt was an understatement. He'd been crushed when Locky assumed he was ready to move Eric into his bed. Maybe it was foolish thinking, but he thought he and Locky were really starting to build something solid. What did it say for their relationship if one misconstrued sentence could derail them? "Like I said, we need to talk, but not today."

"Nervous?" Locky asked, taking the keys out of the ignition.

"Terrified. I haven't been face to face with Jigger since I confronted him in the alley that night." Becket usually talked to Eric about his fears regarding Jigger because he knew how much it upset Locky, but he knew Locky would see them first-hand in less than two hours.

"I know, and I'll be there for you." Locky grinned. "And you'll have three strong brothers who would be only too happy to take Jigger down if he looks at you funny."

"Huh?"

"You're family support team has arrived and are presently sitting in that restaurant waiting for you to get your ass out of the car."

"Stop shittin' me." Becket refused to believe his brothers, the same brothers who practically ignored him growing up, would fly all the way to Idaho. "They know I'm not testifying, right?"

"They know, but they thought you might need them around anyway," Locky explained.

Becket gave Locky another quick kiss before opening his door. "Then what're we waiting for?"

Laughing, Locky got out and joined Becket at the front of the car. "I called the owner and told him about the situation and he said he'd set us up in the banquet room."

"Cool." Becket entered the restaurant and stepped up to the hostess stand. "Do you have three big farm boys in a banquet room?"

The pretty college student smiled. "They belong to you?"

"Kinda."

She pointed towards a room with slatted swinging doors. "Right through there, Mr Regent."

Becket pointed to Locky. "He's Mr Regent, I'm just his faithful sidekick, Becket."

Walking towards the room, Locky bumped against Becket's shoulder. "I think that's the first time I've seen you flirt with a girl."

Becket backhanded Locky playfully on the stomach. "I wasn't flirting. I was spreading my charm."

The moment Becket laid eyes on his three brothers, tears started to form. He still couldn't believe they were here. Like a kid at Christmas, Becket screamed in excitement and ran to his brothers.

Cade was the first to get to him. He scooped Becket up in a tight embrace. "How're you doing?"

"I'm so much better now." Becket wrapped his arms around Cade's muscular neck and hugged him. For years he'd wished he had a loving relationship with his brothers and knowing it was finally happening was overwhelming. He felt a tear escape and quickly dashed it away before anyone else could see it. "I love you," he whispered in Cade's ear.

Cade set Becket's feet back on the floor before releasing him. "You, too."

They weren't the words Becket had hoped for, but they were close enough. He moved to Nic and Del, receiving hugs from both before sitting down. Staring at his brothers around the table, Becket shook his head. "I still can't believe you're here. Who's taking care of the farm?"

"Corn's in, so at the moment it's just a matter of looking after the animals. Scotty agreed to do that for me, Nic and Del and Dad's taking care of his own," Cade explained.

"Is Dad well enough?" Becket had heard very little about his folks since returning home. Evidently, Cade had spoken with Nic and Del and they were giving their parents a wide berth for the time being.

"He was determined to work two days after he got home from the hospital, and no one could tell him otherwise," Nic began.

"So, we said to hell with it. If he dies feeding the cows, he goes doing what he loved most," Del finished.

"And Mom?" Becket was hesitant to ask.

Nic, Cade and Del exchanged glances. "She's Mom, nothing's really changed on her part," Cade finally answered for the group. He grabbed a chip from the bowl and dunked it in a smaller bowl of salsa. "Julie and I are fixing to separate. It'll take a little more time before she can find a place, but we're both at peace with the decision."

"How's Dad feel about that?" Becket was proud of Cade for finally standing up for himself.

"Not much he can say that I care to hear. Since we're all equal partners in the farm, and I own my house, he'll have to learn to deal with it or move." Cade shut up when a waiter came into the room, carrying water glasses for Becket and Locky.

It was two weeks before Becket's twenty-first birthday, but he really wanted a margarita. Unfortunately, there was no way in hell he'd be able to sneak one with four watch dogs surrounding him. Even worse, Cade and Locky both ordered one while Becket was stuck drinking iced tea. "This sucks."

"You're almost there," Locky soothed.

"Nic has something to tell ya," Cade announced.

"Yeah? What's that?" Becket put a hand on Locky's thigh to let him know he wasn't purposely trying to ignore him.

"Lisa's pregnant," Nic said with pride. "We just cleared our first trimester."

"Congratulations," Becket and Locky replied in unison.

The waiter brought their drinks and took their order before disappearing again. Becket was surprised when Cade slid his margarita in front of Becket. "Happy pre-Birthday."

"You mean it?" Becket picked up the glass and looked at Locky. "I haven't had alcohol since…"

Locky seemed to know exactly what Becket was thinking. "Then it's good to have your first surrounded by people who love you."

Becket held his breath. It was the closest Locky had ever come to saying, 'I love you.' He continued to gaze into Locky's sexy green eyes, hoping for more, but Locky quickly looked away.

Uncomfortable, Becket licked the rim of his glass and drank almost a third of his margarita in one swallow.

"That's a good way to get brain freeze," Del teased.

"Yeah, well, maybe a brain freeze today wouldn't be so bad," Becket mumbled.

Cade shifted in his chair. "Have you heard anything about how it went this morning?"

Becket shook his head. "Eric called, but he hasn't sat in on anything so far. He said the less time he has to spend in the same room with Paul Williams, the better."

"Eric, that's the victim, right?" Nic asked.

"*One* of them," Becket corrected. "But he's the one the case is built around."

"Locky told me the two of you have become friends." Cade reached over and stole Becket's water glass.

"Yeah, he's a good guy. Going through a lot of crap right now, but he'll be okay." Becket took another drink.

"I'm sorry," Nic apologised. "That's why I'm usually the quiet one. I always seem to stick my foot in my mouth when I open it."

"It's okay." Becket tried to brush off the sting of Nic's words. "I guess it's just hard because even though Jigger will probably be found guilty, he'll be serving time for what he did to Eric. What about what he did to me? I get so mad when I think about it, but what makes it worse is knowing it's my own damn fault. I should've been strong enough to go to the police that morning Jack found me on the porch."

Locky's arms wrapped around Becket's waist. "The important thing is you finally got there. You stood up and acknowledged it to yourself and the police."

"Thanks, babe. I know you're trying to make me feel better, but we both know it's the truth. It's hard, but I'm learning to live with the decision I made that morning." Becket gave Locky a quick kiss. He had a confession to make that had plagued him with guilt ever since it had happened. He wasn't sure that a lunch with his brothers was the right place for it, but he couldn't go to the courthouse without coming clean. "I met with Fallon this morning after my test."

Locky's jaw immediately clenched. "You did? I thought you were at school meeting with one of your professors and instead I find out you went to talk to that asshole?"

Becket turned in his chair to face Locky, putting his back to his brothers. "I didn't go to the club if that's what you're worrying about. We met at that little diner by the college. I needed to explain to him why I'm still avoiding him. I knew I'd see him today in court, and I didn't want it to be our first time since that night."

"And?" Locky prompted.

"And," Becket began, "I couldn't believe how bad he looked. In a weird way, I guess he's also one of Jigger's victims. Fallon trusted that fucker and it's really shaken him up. So, I let him off the hook for what happened to me. After all, his only crime was trusting his employee to pour drinks and not spike them."

Locky was visibly upset for several torturous moments, but his expression eventually softened. "If it made you feel better, I'm okay with it."

Becket kissed Locky again. "Don't take this the wrong way, but I'd have been glad I did it even if you weren't okay with it. I did it for Fallon and me. I know I should've told you before I met him, but I was afraid you'd talk me out of it, and it was really important to me."

"What's taking the food so long?" Del asked from the opposite end of the table.

Becket knew he was making everyone else uncomfortable, but he still had one thing left on his mind. "I love you," he confessed to Locky. "And I need you to remember that."

Tears filled Locky's eyes. "I love you, too," he said for the first time.

The kiss they shared went deeper than any of the others since they'd arrived at the restaurant. The only reason they broke apart was because Nic and Del started making exaggerated gagging noises.

Becket pulled back and grinned. "We'll discuss this later."

* * * *

Becket walked into the courtroom with his head held high. People who loved him surrounded him and no matter what kind of look Jigger gave him, Becket knew he was safe. Locky led him to a bench towards the back of the room, but Becket shook his head. "I promised Eric I'd sit where he could see me when he's up there."

With a nod of acceptance, Locky found the five of them spots, two seats on the second row close to Jack and Charlie and three on the third. "Okay?"

Becket glanced over his shoulder at the trio of strong farm boys. "Oh, yeah, perfect."

They all stood while the judge entered. Becket watched the jury closely as the prosecutor presented his opening statement to the court. He kept hoping to spot a grimace or at least a twinge on the faces of the assembled men and women, but he was sadly disappointed. They just sat there, staring at the prosecutor. Even the graphic details of Eric's injuries, including the amount of blood lost due to internal injuries wasn't enough to prompt much emotion from the jury.

Becket wasn't the only one squirming in their seat as the prosecution continued to lay out their case. It was two hours into the afternoon session before they finally called Eric Kloiber to the stand.

The doors behind Becket opened and Eric walked into the courtroom. He paused as he passed and Becket gave his new friend a reassuring smile. Eric met Becket's gaze for a few brief moments before continuing onto the stand.

Becket tucked his foot under him to raise himself up another few inches, hoping it would help Eric in some small way. Although the new position helped Becket see Eric, it also gave him a better view of Jigger. He turned his head, refusing to look at the man who had caused so many people so much pain. He returned his attention to Eric. *You can do it*, he silently told his friend.

During Eric's testimony and subsequent cross-examination, Becket concentrated on keeping his expression serene. Eric had already told Becket most of what he was now relaying to the court, so Becket was able to maintain his composure for Eric's sake.

As Eric was questioned, the prosecution entered his clothes into evidence. Although Jigger thought he was playing it smart by using a condom before he'd traded for an oversized dildo, the hospital had detected semen splatters on Eric's jeans. Evidently, Jigger had been in such a rush to rid himself of the condom, he'd inadvertently spilled its contents before disposing of it.

At one point in the trial, a man sitting behind Jigger, made a snide comment when Eric testified that without having been given the drug he would've never agreed to sex with Jigger.

Becket leaned over to Locky. "Who is he?"

"Jigger's brother," Locky answered. "A doctor. I read in the paper that the police are investigating him, too."

Becket had made a point of not reading the local paper since returning to school. The less he knew about Jigger the better, in his opinion.

Jigger's defence attorney was brutal, and by the end, Eric was visibly shaking. Becket tried to imagine what Eric was going through. It had been hard enough answering questions for the police and prosecutor. He couldn't imagine being cross-examined by the high-priced piece of scum who'd been hired by Jigger's family to defend their wayward son.

By the time Eric was finished, it was too late in the day to continue. The judge set the continuation for the following day and adjourned the court.

Becket stood and stretched his arms over his head before turning to face his brothers. All three had obviously been shaken by what they'd heard. He knew his brothers had been picturing him up on the stand instead of Eric, but he wondered what he could possibly say…

Locky put his hand on Becket's shoulder and gestured for him to follow the crowd out of the courtroom. Once they were in the lobby, Becket excused himself. "I'm supposed to meet Eric in the bathroom. I'll be right back."

"Ask him if he'd like to join us for dinner," Cade offered.

"Will do."

After Becket ran off to find Eric, Locky led the rest of them to one of the large columns, out of the way. "You guys okay?"

Cade shook his head. "After hearing that, I doubt I'll ever forget it." Tears filled his eyes. "The thought of Becket going through something like that alone will haunt me forever. If I'd have been a better brother…"

"Don't," Locky said, cutting Cade off. "Thinking that way won't help, believe me. And just so you know, Becket didn't suffer the injuries Eric did. I'm not downplaying what he endured in any way, but at least knowing that might help some."

"I feel sorry for that kid." Cade jammed his hands in the front pockets of his dress pants.

Locky nodded. "I think if it hadn't been for Becket, Eric would've quit school by now. He's a senior with eight and a half months to go and he was close to throwing it all away because of that nasty fucker."

Cade rocked back and forth on his heels. "I guess taking care of Mom all those years taught him how to deal with people who need help."

"Maybe so." Locky waved to Jack, who was leading Charlie out of the courtroom. In an effort to fill the silence, Locky explained to Becket's brothers who they were.

"You should invite them to dinner with us," Nic suggested.

"I could, but they wouldn't come. Jack cooks dinner every night except Saturday and Sunday for everyone in the house, so they'll need to get back. You should stop by after we eat though and meet them."

"We will," Cade agreed. He turned sideways, shielding Locky from Nic and Del. "Promise me you'll keep an eye on Becket. I don't want to go home after all this is over and have to worry about whether or not he's safe."

"I'd defend him with my life," Locky replied in all honesty. "He means everything to me."

Cade chuckled. "Yeah, I got that from the little exchange at lunch."

"Good. Then you know my intentions are completely honourable towards him." It wasn't the same as asking the eldest Chandler brother for Becket's hand in marriage, but it was as close as he'd ever get.

* * * *

"Do you think the judge will find him guilty?" Becket whispered.

Locky reached over and held Becket's hand in the darkness of his bedroom. "Without a doubt. The evidence is there, and after the detective testifies tomorrow, I think the only real question left will be how much time Jigger has to serve."

Will James had been the detective in charge of the case against Jigger since the beginning, and although Locky didn't like him for the harsh way he'd questioned Becket, he did trust the man's abilities. He had to believe Will had the case tied up tight.

Becket rolled to his side. "Do you really love me?"

Locky pulled Becket down into his arms. Their mutual proclamation of love at lunch had surprised him, but he knew it had been a long time coming. "With all my heart. I didn't want to tell you because I didn't want you to feel pressured."

"Why would I feel pressured? You're the gentlest man I've ever known. You give me everything I could ever hope to have."

"I don't ever want you to feel tied down." Locky scraped his lower lip with his teeth. "According to my mother, my love is smothering, and I don't want you to feel that way."

"You're right, you're mom's a bitch." Becket leaned in for a deep kiss. "Just so you know, you can tie me down anytime as long as I can do the same thing to you."

It was a typical statement from Becket. Locky had learnt soon after they started sleeping together that Becket tried to diffuse tense or uncomfortable situations with humour, and more often than not, it worked.

They settled into a comfortable silence. Holding Becket in his arms as he drifted to sleep was Locky's favourite part of the day. There was something so honest and pure in Becket's love that Locky prayed he'd never have to live another moment without it.

Locky still thought of Steven, the young man who'd died in his arms, from time to time. Locky may not have been able to save Steven, but because of Steven's death, Locky was making a difference in the lives of young gay men just like him. Earlier that evening, he had spoken to Charlie about moving Eric into the room Becket rarely used. Charlie had been all for it after, once again, asking Locky to quell the noises that tended to come from his apartment. Both Locky and Becket had agreed to figure out a way if it meant getting Eric out of the dorm and into BK.

"You asleep?"

"No." Locky kissed the top of Becket's head. "Just wondering how much it would cost to have this room soundproofed."

"Room? I say go for the whole apartment. I've been dying to get fucked over that little kitchen table you have in the other room."

"Really?" All kinds of possibilities ran through Locky's mind. He threw back the covers and sat up. "You grab the pillow to scream into, and I'll get the supplies."

THE INJUSTICE OF BEING

Chapter One

Eric Kloiber concentrated on the small tag of skin he was desperately trying to remove from the corner of his well-bitten nail. He wasn't normally a nail-biter, but his sore, bloody cuticles had suffered as much as his head and heart since the night he had been drugged and raped.

"Something's wrong," Eric mumbled to himself.

"Excuse me?"

Eric glanced at the police officer posted outside the courtroom door. "Sorry. I was..." He shook his head. "Never mind."

The officer went back to his post, leaving Eric to wonder what the hell was going on. What should have been a speedy trial had turned into the hardest two weeks of his life. After his initial testimony, the defence had suddenly produced a copy of the prescription Jigger had used to get the Rohypnol in the first place. According to the defence attorney, Jigger had been prescribed the sleeping aid because of his odd employment hours. Coincidentally, the prescription had been signed by Jigger's brother, Dr

Adam Williams. The prosecutor argued that the evidence should have been presented to them in the discovery phase of the hearing, but the defence claimed they'd only just obtained the copy from a mail-in pharmacy Jigger used.

The whole thing was fucked up. Even worse, everyone had told him it should be a quick deliberation for the jury, but that hadn't turned out to be true either. Six days. What the hell was there to discuss in an open-and-shut case for six fucking days?

Eric stood and began to pace back and forth in the marbled hall. He wished he'd asked Becket to sit with him while they waited for the jury's decision, but he couldn't bring himself to do that. Becket had attended every day of the trial with his boyfriend, Locky. It wouldn't have been fair to ask him to miss the verdict. Even though Jigger was being tried for Eric's rape, Becket had also been one of Jigger's victims. Unfortunately, Becket had kept his rape a secret until it was too late to obtain the evidence needed for a conviction.

The heavy door to the courtroom opened and Eric stopped walking at the explosion of voices filtering into the hall. Cries of outrage from several familiar voices took Eric's breath away. He lowered himself back to the bench and stared up at the detective who had been in charge of the investigation. Will James' light brown hair, was longer than it had been at the start of the investigation, but Eric assumed his attention had been too focused on putting Jigger away to worry about something as trivial as his appearance. The grim expression on Will's face seemed to confirm Eric's biggest fear.

"Not guilty," Eric surmised.

Will nodded and sat beside Eric, his much larger frame making Eric feel small and vulnerable. "Not guilty on the drug charge. They couldn't reach an agreement on the rape charge. The judge had no choice but to issue a mistrial."

"Mistrial." As he said the word, Eric's body began to go numb. "What exactly does that mean?"

Will rested his forearms on his thighs and rubbed his hands together. "The prosecution will take a second look at the case and decide whether or not to retry it."

"You mean they might not?"

"Trials are expensive. Evidently we didn't have enough to convince this jury." Will sighed. "Sorry, kid, but I honestly don't know what Byron will decide."

Misplaced anger filled Eric. Whether he was mad at Byron Long, the prosecutor, or the whole fucking judicial system, he didn't know or care, but he lashed out at Will. "I'm not a kid. You don't go through what I've been through and remain a damn kid."

Will sat up. "You're right. I apologise."

The heavy door opened again as people began to leave the courtroom. The last place Eric wanted to be was at the centre of his friends' pity. "I gotta get outta here."

Before Will or anyone else could stop him, Eric jumped to his feet and ran down the hall. He considered hiding out in the bathroom, but he knew that would be the first place Becket would search. Instead, he ran down the wide staircase, taking the steps two at a time. He slowed to a walk as he got to the security station and nodded to the guards before exiting the building.

Eric didn't realise until he was two blocks down the street that Will hadn't told him whether or not Jigger would be freed. "Fuck!"

* * * *

"How the hell did that happen?" Will asked Byron as the prosecutor left the courtroom.

"Not enough concrete evidence."

"Jigger's an ex-con. His sperm was found on Eric's jeans. Eric was sitting at the bar being attended by Jigger at the end of the night, and Rohypnol was found behind the bar, in Jigger's work locker *and* in his home." Will took a deep breath as he continued to tick items off on his fingers. "Not to mention the array of sexual tools found in the trunk of his car."

"But no one saw *Mr Williams* give Eric the drug or leave the club with him, and since Eric can't remember, it simply isn't enough," Byron explained. "And going to prison for six months at the age of eighteen for stealing a car to go joyriding with his friends is a long way from a hardened criminal past."

Will's hands curled into fists. It wasn't the first time Byron had subtly reprimanded Will for his use of Paul Williams' nickname. "Are you going to retry him?"

Byron stopped walking and turned to face Will. "Not unless I have more evidence. You get me that, and I'll do my part to get a conviction. In the meantime, Mr Williams will be released on bond, pending another trial." He leaned towards Will. "If you get me something more to take it to trial."

The thought of Jigger out on the streets brought Eric's safety to mind. "What about Eric, can he take out a restraining order or something?"

"The judge issued Mr Williams several warnings before he set bail. Unless he defies those warnings, Eric shouldn't need to petition for a restraining order."

Will inwardly groaned. The pressure to produce more evidence was overwhelming. Not only was Byron counting on him, but he knew Eric's faith in the justice system hinged on a conviction. It was something Will didn't know if he could deliver, because despite his skills as an investigator, he couldn't produce evidence out of thin air. Hell, he'd worked his ass off building the case in the first place. He'd questioned every person Eric remembered seeing in the bar the night he'd been drugged and raped and…nothing. He hadn't come up with a goddamn person who remembered seeing anything unusual the night Eric was left bleeding in the lobby of the dorm. It was something that had always bothered him.

After glancing at his watch, Byron set his briefcase on the floor and shrugged into his beige trench coat. "I'm due at the office. By the way, the jury was locked at nine to three. We're almost there, but not quite."

Will nodded as Byron picked up his briefcase and started down the steps. He should get back to the station, but before he dug back into the files, he needed to make sure Eric was okay. No, he admonished himself. The best way for him to assuage his guilt was to do his job. Holding Eric's hand would make Will feel better but not because it was the right thing to do. It wasn't the time to be selfish.

Before leaving the courthouse, he stopped in front of the Lady Justice statue in the Grand Rotunda. He'd always loved the statue and had spent hours as a kid looking up at it in awe.

"Bad day?"

Will turned to find his father, Henry. Although they resembled each other in hair colour and height, Henry's rounded stomach was a testament to years of eating Will's mom's cooking. He pointed at the statue. "She let me down today."

Laying a hand on Will's shoulder, his dad shook his head. "I've cleaned this building for thirty-seven years. Watched all kinds of men and women stand right where you're standing and curse that lady." He turned to stare at Will. "You know what they all had in common?"

"They lost," Will guessed.

"Just because someone doesn't get the verdict they want, doesn't mean it wasn't the right one."

Will looked away from the statue and studied his father for several moments. His dad loved the law, was fascinated by the entire process and even after thirty-seven years of sitting in on trial proceedings every break and lunch hour, Henry James' faith in the system had never wavered. "Did you catch any of the trial?"

"Sure," his dad replied.

Although his captain would probably kill him, Will trusted his dad over all others. "What went wrong?"

His father shrugged. "I didn't know Mr Williams. Byron Long sat a handsome man in front of five women and seven men and tried to convince them he'd committed a heinous act, but he didn't have the evidence to back it up."

Although his dad was using Byron as the scapegoat, Will knew his father was talking directly to him. "What would've convinced you?"

"History. Did he torture cats, look into the bedroom windows of his friends? A man who would drug and rape young men didn't start overnight. If I was sittin' on that jury, I'd want to know for sure that the man I'm putting away is bad." Will's dad grinned. "So prove to me he's a bad apple and a danger to society."

Will had checked for priors on Jigger, but he hadn't dug very deeply into the guy's past. His attention had been on Eric and making the entire process as easy as he could on the guy. Not that he would ever cross the line with a victim, but he'd admitted to himself shortly after meeting Eric that there was something special about the young man.

Fuck. It wasn't Byron's, Lady Justice's or the jury's fault the trial had ended the way it had. The majority of the blame could be squarely put on his shoulders, but he refused to carry the entire load. Vince, his captain, had assigned the investigation to Will because of its nature. He didn't feel the other cops would be comfortable with the victim or the subject matter, and he'd been right. Still, Vince had scrutinised the time Will spent interviewing people who were at the club and dorm the night of Eric's rape. "I don't know how much more time Vince'll let me spend on this," Will admitted.

"It won't really matter if it's important enough to you." His dad met Will's gaze. "Is it?"

Will thought of Eric and his struggle to find balance in his life after being outed in such a horrific and public way. "I think Eric needs it. I'm not sure he'll be able to move on if we don't get a conviction."

"That's not what I asked. Is. It. Important. To. You?" his dad asked again, stressing each word individually.

Will had been one of the lucky few. He'd come out to his parents at a young age without fear of reprisals, so he knew what his dad was really asking. He ran his hands through his hair, feeling the slight curls wrap around his fingers as he did. "Yeah, I like him, but it would be unethical to take advantage of the situation."

His dad grinned. "So do what you have to do to nail that sonofabitch, and the two of you can meet on a level playing field."

Will didn't even know if Eric would be interested in going out with him. "He's been through a lot."

"Of course he has. I didn't say it would be easy, but I've never known you to back away from something you wanted just because it wasn't."

Hell, he needed to get away from his dad before he talked him into running to Eric and confessing everything. "I'd better go. It seems I have a past to dig into."

* * * *

After leaving Becket a message on his cell, Eric leaned back against a tree in a nearby nature park and took another swig from his bottle of Wild Turkey. He grimaced and did an all-over body shake as the strong whisky slid down his throat and burned a path to his stomach. He'd purposely waited until dinnertime at BK House to call, knowing Charlie's no-phones-at-the-table rule would save him from actually having to talk to a person. He may not yet officially live at BK, but he was still expected to obey the house rules.

Although he didn't want company, he didn't want his friends to worry either. He stared at the phone in his hand and wished he could call home, his real home, not the one he'd manufactured for himself at BK. Unfortunately, Jigger had not only taken his virginity, he'd taken his family.

Eric tossed his phone onto the ground and upended the bottle again, going through the same grimace as before. Why in the world did people drink this stuff for pleasure? He had one goal at the moment, to get drunk enough to pass out.

The night he'd been found in the dorm lobby, unconscious and bleeding, the police had contacted his parents. Surprisingly, his mother and father had immediately flown to Idaho to be at his bedside, but everything changed the minute they heard he'd been in a gay bar before he'd been raped. Put on the spot, Eric finally confessed to being a homosexual, something unforgivable in his parents' eyes. *Fucking Southern Baptists.* Just as quickly as they'd come, his parents had left, telling Eric he would no longer be welcome in their home until he gave up his shameful lifestyle and returned to the church he'd been raised in.

Eric's only saving grace was that his money for college came from a small trust left to him by his grandmother Kloiber. Otherwise, he'd have lost absolutely everything the night Jigger had drugged him.

Jigger. Testifying against the man who had raped him was the hardest thing Eric had ever done. He'd barely spoken to Jigger that night at the bar other than ordering a couple of beers. What was it about him that made Jigger believe he would be an easy target? Eric hated to admit it, but Jigger was incredibly sexy. It had been Jigger's swagger and cheesy come-ons that had made him unattractive to Eric that night.

Something flashed in Eric's mind, a mental picture of waking up as Jigger carefully placed him in the backseat of a car. Eric sucked in a breath. It was the first memory he'd been able to conjure up since that night. Would it help? He wondered if the detective and the prosecutor would believe him.

He tucked the bottle of bourbon between his crossed legs and found his phone in a shallow pile of leaves. With shaking hands, he called Detective James.

"James," Will answered.

"It's Eric. Eric Kloiber. I remembered something." Eric realised his words were slurred due to the alcohol, but he hoped the detective wouldn't hold that against him.

It took a moment for the detective to answer. "Are you drunk?"

"Maybe—yeah, probably, but that's not why I called. I remember Jigger putting me in a car."

"Where're you at?"

"Twin Creeks Nature Preserve. I'm off one of the hiking trails on the south end."

The detective sighed. "It's getting dark. Stay where you are and I'll come get you."

Eric shook his head. "No, that's not why I called. If I needed a ride, I'd call Becket or Jack. I just wanted you to know that I remembered something that you might be able to use."

"And I will, but your safety is my first priority." A car door slammed in the background. "I'll be there in ten minutes."

Eric leaned his head back against the tree. "I don't want you to pick me up. There's nowhere I want to go. The thought of seeing pity in my friends' eyes is enough to keep me here all night."

"Worry isn't the same as pity, and I'm not about to let you sleep in the goddamn park," Will growled.

Eric took another drink from the bottle. Surprisingly, the bourbon was starting to go down much easier. From the tone of the detective's voice, Eric knew there was no dissuading him. "Fine. I can see the footbridge from where I am. You want me to meet you there?"

"No. I don't want you anywhere near the water if you're drunk. Just keep your little ass right where it is. I'll find you."

The call dropped suddenly, which wasn't surprising given the terrain of the area. Eric shoved the phone in the pocket of his blue dress shirt and closed his eyes. He couldn't keep the goofy grin off his face. The detective had called his ass little. Did that mean he'd noticed it before? Eric didn't know many straight guys who commented on the size of another man's ass, which led him to believe Will James might just be gay. "Cool."

Growing up in a town of just over four thousand people, it was natural for Eric to lust over straight guys, hell, that was all that had been around. So he hadn't thought a thing about it when he'd had those familiar butterflies in his stomach whenever Will was around. He'd just chalked it up to one more unrequited attraction, but if the detective was gay, that put things in a whole different perspective.

Eric's cock began to harden, surprising him even further. Since the rape, his sex drive had almost been nonexistent, not that he'd ever done much about it in the first place, but he used to have a fairly good relationship with his right hand. After being released from the hospital, even jacking off didn't hold the appeal it once had.

Eric reached down and rubbed the heel of his hand against the hardening bulge in his khaki pants. He slowly unzipped them and reached inside, sighing at the first hard squeeze of his cock in ages. He was working up a righteous climax when the sound of Will's voice shattered the moment.

"Eric!"

Shit. Shit. Shit. Eric quickly released his cock and carefully eased the zipper closed. He must be drunker than he'd thought. "I'm here," he called back.

Dressed in a pair of faded jeans and an old red sweatshirt, Will left the hiking trail and made his way towards Eric. It was the first time Eric had seen the detective without his usual cheap wrinkled suit, and damn the man looked good. He glanced down at the front of his tented pants and sighed. The bottle of whisky was all he had to hide his condition. He grabbed the bottle and rested it against his fly. Fuck, the pressure felt good.

Will came to a stop and bent over to rest his hands on his knees, taking deep breaths. It was obvious Will had run the entire trail trying to reach him. Something about the thought wrapped warmth around Eric. "You really didn't need to come out here. I'd have made it back to BK eventually."

Will plopped down beside Eric. "The temperature's supposed to drop overnight."

With his thin frame and only a borrowed navy blazer to keep him warm, Eric knew he'd have been in trouble if he passed out. "Oh," was all he could think to say.

When Will reached for Eric's crotch, Eric held his breath. He was sadly disappointed when Will wrapped his hand around the neck of the Wild Turkey bottle instead of what was proudly on display underneath.

Will paused as he lifted the bottle off Eric's erection. He turned his head away after several seconds and set the whisky on the ground between them. "You have a cap for this?"

Seriously? Eric couldn't believe Will was going to act like he hadn't just been staring at his boner. Had he been wrong about Will? Maybe the ass comment he'd made earlier was just chatter. Eric looked around the area, idly searching the multicoloured leaves that littered the ground. "Should be around here somewhere."

Again, Will started to reach for Eric but pulled his hand back, obviously having second thoughts. "I think it's on the other side of your leg."

Eric picked up the cap and held it aloft. "Well, what d'ya know."

Will took the cap and replaced it on the bottle. "So tell me about this memory again."

Eric had almost forgotten why he'd called Will in the first place. "Like I said, it just came to me. I remembered opening my eyes and seeing Jigger's face when he loaded me in the car."

"I don't suppose you remember anything else, like where you were or if he'd already raped you?"

Eric bit his bottom lip and shook his head. "No, just him." He recalled the expression on Jigger's face. "I don't think he was happy though. He had that tense bulging jaw-thing guys get when they're upset."

Will picked up the bottle and got to his feet. He held his hand out to Eric. "Let's get out of here before they close the park."

Eric took Will's hand. Evidently, the fact that he finally had a memory of that night meant little to the detective. "That's not going to help the case, is it?"

Will pulled Eric to his feet and shook his head. "Honestly, I don't know. It won't be enough, but maybe if we're lucky, more stuff will start to come back to you."

It had been months since the rape and the one memory was all that Eric had. "It was hard getting up on the witness stand and talking about what happened, I mean, you know, the parts I remember." He blew out a breath, smelling the alcohol that he'd drunk. "I know it's not fair to you or Mr Long, but I don't want to remember exactly what happened to me that night." Eric shoved his hands in his front pockets and started towards the path. "I just don't."

Chapter Two

Will closed the passenger door and walked to the nearest trashcan. He tossed the half-empty bottle of whisky away and returned to the car. Like a typical drunk, Eric had gone from horny to depressed in a matter of minutes.

Sliding behind the steering wheel, Will glanced over at his passenger. Eric's shoulder-length brown hair had fallen across his face, shielding his thickly lashed eyes from view. Will took a moment to appreciate Eric's lean body. At least with his sudden sullen mood Eric's obvious erection had subsided. *Good.* It had been all too tempting and oddly exciting. Eric was the forbidden fruit that he knew he couldn't have, but wanted anyway.

"Do you want me to drop you at BK House or the dorm?" Will knew Eric had been sleeping in Becket's old room lately. It was a shame the other students in Eric's dorm had given him a hard time about his recently discovered sexual preference, but Will was glad Eric had found a spot in BK House.

"Neither," Eric mumbled.

"I have to take you somewhere."

Eric grinned for the first time since they'd started back down the trail. "You can take me to your place."

"Tempting." He bit his bottom lip, his gaze captured by Eric's. "Really tempting, actually, but I can't until we close the investigation."

Eric turned sideways in the seat. "You mean it?"

The mood in the car had turned serious, and Will was suddenly put on the spot. As much as he would love to pull Eric into his arms, he couldn't. Worse, if he failed to get the evidence needed to convict Jigger, he'd never be able to do all the things he'd been dreaming about because deep down, he knew Eric would never forgive him.

"Ask me again after we put Jigger away," Will finally replied.

"Why do we have to wait? If I'm into you and you're into me. Isn't that enough for you?"

It was more than enough, but Will had to keep his head. "Sure, it's enough for me, the man, but I'm the lead investigator and if Jigger's lawyer discovered we were seeing each other socially, he'd have the case thrown out. Besides, I could lose my job, and being a cop means everything to me."

Eric tilted his head back and closed his eyes. "In other words, Jigger's fucking me again."

Will ground his teeth together in frustration. "The system's not perfect, but it helps more than it hurts. Don't give up, or Jigger'll win."

Eric kicked out at Will's dashboard.

"And don't fuck up my car," Will added. He understood why Eric was frustrated, but if Eric let his emotions control him, it could lead him down the wrong path. Will tried to soften the admonishment by reaching out. He squeezed Eric's shoulder before releasing his hold. "Have faith in me. I'll get what I need to tie this case up so tight the jury won't have a damn thing to argue over."

Eric opened his eyes. "I hope you're right, because I don't think I can go through this again."

* * * *

Although Eric still wasn't completely comfortable at BK House, it was a heck of a lot better than living in the dorm with his homophobic ex-roommate, Ira. His new roommate, Rusty Bonham, was a freshman, and far too twitchy for Eric's peace of mind. Cute in a little kid sort of way, Rusty rarely spoke and when he did, his voice was so soft it was hard to understand him.

Eric entered their shared room and took off the borrowed jacket, hoping Rusty wouldn't ask him about the trial. He'd managed to get into the house and up the stairs without anyone seeing him and wanted to lay low for the rest of the evening.

Rusty glanced up from his advanced physics textbook. Seriously, what freshman signed up for advanced physics? It hadn't taken Eric long to discover his roommate was also a brainiac.

"Hi," Rusty greeted.

Eric nodded, but didn't speak. Maybe if he kept silent, it would give Rusty the clue that he didn't want to talk. He hung up the jacket, but realised it would need to be cleaned before returning.

Rusty went back to his textbook without another word, and Eric was suddenly glad he'd landed him to share a room with. He grabbed his towel and shaving kit and headed to the communal bathroom.

Still tipsy, Eric waited until he closed the curtain on the small dressing room outside the shower stall to strip out of his clothes. He heard the bathroom door open and quickly turned on the water, hoping to avoid conversation.

"I know you're in here," Becket said from outside the curtain.

Eric stepped under the spray and closed the second curtain, putting two plastic barriers between him and Becket. Of course it didn't offer him any protection from Becket's voice, but he felt safer knowing Becket couldn't see him.

"It sucks," Becket said.

Understatement of the year. Eric built up a good lather in the palms of his hands before transferring it to his body. His cock, which had been craving attention earlier, now hung flaccid as he scrubbed himself.

"I'm not leaving," Becket announced.

Eric rolled his eyes. Becket was the closest thing he had to a true friend. He'd had a few buddies in his hometown, but he'd always kept the secret of who he really was from them, therefore, he never really thought of them as friends, just people to hang out with. Becket was different. Not only had he suffered a similar attack at Jigger's hands, but he had reached out to Eric like no one else ever had. *I owe him.*

"I don't want to talk about it," Eric finally said.

"So, let's talk about something else. Where were you this afternoon?"

"Getting drunk at Twin Peaks Nature Preserve." Eric tried, once again, to get his cock interested but failed. He gave up and turned around to wash his hair.

"With who?" Becket asked.

"With myself. Well, for a while, then I called Will."

"Detective James?" Becket questioned. "Why would you call him instead of me?"

Eric finished washing his hair before answering. He turned off the shower and lifted the towel off its hook. After a quick rub dry, Eric put on a pair of sweats and an oversized T-shirt. Barefoot, he slid back the outer curtain. He didn't want to talk about the case, hell, at the moment, he didn't even want to fucking think about it, but mostly, he didn't want to talk about his attraction to Will.

Eric decided to change the subject without answering the question. "Did your brothers leave?"

Becket grinned. "Cade's still in town until Sunday if that's what you're asking."

Eric bit his bottom lip. There was something about the way Becket's older brother looked at him that turned Eric on. He was still tipsy enough to take interest in the fact that Cade was still in town.

"Yeah, I guess that's what I wanted to know." He thought of Will, and a moment of guilt hit him square in the gut. *No.* He'd practically thrown himself at Will only to be rebuffed for his efforts under the guise of professionalism. He'd lost his virginity, family and most of his friends to a rapist, so he really didn't have anything else of worth to lose.

"You want his cell phone number?" Becket asked.

Eric walked to the sink and began to comb out his hair. "You trying to set your brother up?"

"Sure. He's into you, I can tell. I don't know what'll happen, though. He's asked his wife for a divorce and he's kinda lusting over his best friend, Scotty, but I don't think they're messing around yet."

At first, Eric was put off by the idea of being some kind of stand-in for Cade's best friend, but he quickly realised Cade would be standing in for Will, so it seemed to make sense.

"Yeah, give me his number."

* * * *

After returning to his house, Will shucked his jeans for a pair of thin sleep pants and settled on the couch with a bottle of lube. Flipping through the channels, he settled on old movie with Cary Grant.

When he pulled his cock out of his pants and poured lube into his hand, it sure as hell wasn't Cary Grant he was thinking about. Eric had really done a number on him, and Will had barely made it to BK House without jumping the younger man's body.

He eased his hand up and down his length, gathering pre-cum on his thumb with a rub to the head on each pass. *Find the evidence, finish the case,* he told himself. It might seem like a weird thing for a man to think about while jacking off, but Will knew he couldn't indulge in the pleasures of Eric's body until he took care of business.

Scooting down to rest his feet on the edge of the coffee table, Will used one hand to manipulate his balls while his other pumped away at this cock. He imagined Eric between his legs, licking his balls and slurping at the pre-cum that coated his dick.

"Ahhh, fuck." It didn't take long for Will to explode. The case and the trial had been long and tiresome and it had been ages since he'd bothered to hook up with someone. It wasn't that he didn't enjoy the occasional one-night stand, but since meeting Eric, Will had absolutely no interest in other men.

The fact that he had met Eric after his brutal rape was probably sick and a little perverted, but there had been something so sincere and afraid in Eric's gaze as he looked up at Will from the hospital bed that Will hadn't been able to get past it.

* * * *

Eric waited in front of BK House for Cade to pick him up. He was beyond nervous and suddenly worried that he was making a mistake. Despite his longing to feel another man's arms around him, he'd never actually done anything while conscious.

Before he could change his mind and run back into the house, a large sedan pulled into the parking lot and stopped in front of him. Eric took a deep breath at the sight of the handsome man behind the wheel. With an upper body sculpted to perfection by the demanding job of a farmer, Cade was fucking gorgeous, and Eric knew he'd be a complete ass to pass up the opportunity in front of him.

Mind made up, Eric walked around to the passenger side and slid in. "Hey. Thanks for picking me up."

"My pleasure," Cade shot back with a grin on his sun bronzed face. "My brothers were driving me crazy, and I'd hoped I'd get to see you again before we left."

Eric buckled his seatbelt as Cade pulled back onto the street. "I didn't plan on seeing anyone, but when Becket cornered me in the bathroom and told me you were still in town…"

Cade reached over and brushed Eric's hand with his. "What do you feel like doing?"

A number of ideas came to Eric's mind, but a part of him was afraid of all of them. "Wanna get some beer and go to the lookout on Summit Road?"

"Sure, if you tell me how to get there."

Eric pointed towards the intersection. "Take a left. There's a liquor store a couple blocks down."

Cade turned the corner. "Any specific brand?" he asked, pulling into the parking lot.

"I'm a student. I'll drink anything wet." Eric snapped his mouth shut, embarrassed by what he'd said.

With a chuckle and shake of his head, Cade opened the car door. "I'll remember that."

Eric stared at Cade's ass as he walked into the store. The tight-fitting Wranglers looked damn good. He sighed, wishing the ass belonged to Will. Eric thumped his head against the back of the seat. He couldn't think like that. It could be months before he got a chance with Will.

Twelve-pack in hand, Cade stepped up to the counter and chatted comfortably with the man behind the register. Eric wondered if it was the country in Cade that made him so damn friendly? When Will chatted, it always came out sounding like an interrogation.

Eric had to hide the big stupid grin on his face whenever he thought of the detective. Will, with his grumpy demeanour and deep voice, was the quintessential cop who had immediately captured Eric's attention. Cade, on the other hand, was kind and sexy, and obviously available, at least for the night. More importantly, from what Becket led him to believe, Cade had only recently come out of the closet, so he probably wasn't as experienced as Will. Eric decided that Cade was the perfect person to teach him a few things. Even if he made a fool of himself, Cade would be gone, and he wouldn't have to be as nervous around Will when the time came to make his move.

The back driver's side door opened and Cade set the beer on the floorboard before getting in behind the wheel. "Where to?"

"Take a left out of the parking lot and go down to Hope Springs and take another left out of town," Eric instructed. He reached for the radio and turned it to a country station.

"You like country?" Cade asked, his voice full of surprise.

"Not really, but I figured you did."

Cade chuckled and turned it up to sing along. "You're right, I do."

As they headed out of town, Eric tried to wrap himself in Cade's good mood, even attempting to sing along on a well-known Kenny Chesney song. Cade playfully punched Eric in the arm. "You're not a music major are you?"

Eric answered by singing louder. "Nope, engineering."

It was the first time since being raped that he'd felt like himself, free of people looking at him with worry and pity, and Eric knew he owed it all to Cade. "Take that," he said, pointing towards a narrow gravel road that led up the side of the large hill. He wouldn't consider it a mountain exactly, but it was tall enough to offer one hell of a view.

"You sure it's okay to be up here?" Cade made a left, following the sharp curves of the serpentine route.

Eric shrugged. "No sign that says we can't."

"Oh shit," Cade said, pulling into the clearing. "This is unbelievable." He parked the car within six feet of the edge and turned off the engine.

"Told ya." Eric opened his door and got out. He stretched his arms over his head and waited for Cade to join him. "Do you think the hood'll hold us?"

Passing Eric a can, Cade shook his head. "I doubt it. Cars aren't made for it nowadays."

With a huff, Eric opened his beer and moved closer to the edge. Between the makeshift parking lot and the drop was a thin strip of grass, well, weeds, but at least they were soft. "Have a seat."

Cade set down the twelve-pack and sat beside Eric. The lights of the city glittered up at them. It was hard for Eric to believe that evil continued to lurk amongst the beauty.

"Hey," Cade said, giving Eric's hand a squeeze. "Don't give up."

Eric leaned against Cade's large frame. "Yeah, I know." He upended his beer and took a long gulp. "I don't want it to follow me tonight."

"Then we won't let it." Cade settled his arm around Eric, bringing him closer to his body.

After several minutes, Eric gathered his courage and looked up at Cade. "I know you have someone back home."

Cade nodded once. "Scotty. I'm afraid I might've screwed that up."

"How so?"

"Waited too long to stand up to my family." Cade looked down and met Eric's gaze. "Scotty's paid the price for my cowardice, and now I'm not sure he'll let me in."

"But that's what you want, right?" Eric pulled out of Cade's embrace and sat up straight.

"More than anything," Cade whispered, more to himself than Eric.

"So why're you up here with me?" Eric had known before calling Cade that they both had someone else they'd rather be with, but he wanted to make sure they were on the same page.

"Lonely, I reckon. You?"

"Same," Eric agreed. "I kinda hoped you'd teach me how to kiss." He turned his head to stare at the lights below. "And other stuff."

Cade lay back and pulled Eric down beside him. "Let's take it one lesson at a time." He sealed his lips over Eric's and slowly led him into a deep kiss. Eric was surprised at how easy it felt to accept Cade's tongue in his mouth. He closed his eyes and tentatively touched his own tongue against Cade's.

Happier than he'd been in a long time, Eric couldn't help but smile. Sure, he knew it wasn't very sexy and definitely showed his inexperience, but he couldn't help himself. When Cade moaned and stroked his tongue against Eric's, Eric giggled. *Fuck.* He couldn't believe he'd just done that.

Cade broke the kiss and reared back. "What's so funny?"

Embarrassed, Eric shook his head. "Nothing's funny, it's...*aarghh.*" Eric groaned and rolled to his back. He stared up at the stars and tried to explain his actions. "I couldn't wait to get out of high school and move away so I could finally feel comfortable in my own skin." He let his voice drift off, still searching for the right words. "That was my first real kiss. Ever."

Eric turned back to Cade, trying to gauge Cade's reaction to the statement. He hoped it went without saying that he'd had no control over what Jigger had done to him. "I'm pretty old to be so inexperienced, huh?"

On his side facing Eric, Cade propped his head on his hand. "I'm a hell of a lot older than you are and although I have more experience, that was the first kiss I've shared with a man since I was a teenager." He leaned in and kissed Eric again, keeping it soft and gentle. He pulled back and his brow furrowed. "I know you were forced out of the closet after what happened, but maybe it's better that way. I was so afraid of what my family would think that I ruined three people's lives because I couldn't come out to them."

Eric nodded in understanding. He'd held a lot of resentment about the way his life had been taken away from him and put on display after the attack, but maybe Cade was right. Despite his desire to enter college an out-and-proud gay man, he'd immediately sunk back into hiding upon meeting his jock roommate. What should've been his exploring years had instead become years of pretending just like he'd done in high school. "All I've ever wanted was to be myself," he admitted.

"And now you are." Cade pushed Eric's hair off his face.

"Yeah, but it cost me my family and most of my friends," Eric pointed out.

"But now you have new friends and you're free to find someone special to share your life with," Cade argued.

Eric was grateful that Cade didn't comment on his homophobic family of assholes even though Becket had surely told him. His thoughts went to Will. It would be naïve of him to assume Will would become the love of his life. "How many guys besides Scotty have you fooled around with?"

Cade shook his head. "None until tonight."

"So why tonight?" A feeling of guilt threatened to overwhelm Eric. Neither of them should be doing what they were doing, and although he longed for physical contact, the only person he really wanted was Will.

Cade sighed and rolled to his back. "I don't know. I guess I wanted to see what it would feel like to be with someone else. To touch another man without some sort of guilt attached."

Eric sat up. It was obvious that the two of them weren't going to go any further than the hot kiss they'd shared moments earlier. "And now that you've thought about it?"

Cade got to his feet and rested his hands on his hips as he stared at the view. "You're a good kisser, experienced or not..."

"But..." Eric prompted when it seemed Cade wouldn't finish his sentence.

Cade drug his hands through his short hair, clearly exasperated. "It's been years since I've kissed Scotty, but I remember it feeling different somehow." He shook his head and turned to stare down at Eric. "It wasn't the way you kissed, so get that notion right out of your head."

Having no experience to draw from, Eric didn't understand. "So why was it different?"

Cade shrugged. "I like you, but that's as far as it goes for me. I loved Scotty, still do."

Eric held out his hand and waited for Cade to help him to his feet. He dusted off his jeans, feeling sad and ashamed. "I think you should go home and do whatever's necessary to get him back."

"I plan to," Cade acknowledged.

Eric loved the kiss he'd shared with Cade, but according to Cade, it would feel even better with Will. His heart started to race just thinking about it. "Would you do me a favour and drop me somewhere on your way back to the hotel?"

"Of course." Cade tilted his head slightly to the side, giving Eric a narrow-eyed gaze. "Who is it that you really want to kiss?"

Eric bit his bottom lip. "Detective James."

Cade frowned. "I didn't get a gay vibe from him. You sure?"

Eric nodded. "Don't let his clothes fool ya, despite those awful suits he wears to court, he's gay. Unfortunately, he won't ask me out until Jigger's behind bars."

"It sucks, but you've gotta see his point."

After reaching into the box, Eric pulled out another beer and held it out. "Want one?"

Cade accepted the can. "Mind if I ask you a personal question?"

Eric chuckled and opened a can for himself. "You just had your tongue down my throat, I think I can handle a question."

"Why'd you go to Fallon's on Fifth that night? I mean, I thought you were still in the closet."

"I was, but I'd just spent an entire summer berating myself for lying to everyone. I got back to school earlier than my roommate and saw an ad for Fallon's place, so I decided to go for it." It was the worst decision Eric had ever made. It wasn't going to the club in the first place that continued to haunt him, but he should've sat at a table instead of the bar. Maybe if he'd listened to his initial instincts and kept to the shadows, Jigger would never have noticed him.

"Shit."

"Yeah," Eric agreed. Instead of nudging him out of the closet, the rape had thrust him headfirst into a hellish nightmare he often thought he'd never wake from.

"The really stupid part is that I don't think I would've gone to the police if the hospital hadn't called them." Eric took a drink of his beer. "Sometimes I think Becket was lucky."

"I think Becket would agree with you." Cade picked up the twelve-pack and settled it against his side. "You sure you want me to drop you by that detective's place?"

"Yeah, if you don't mind?" Eric finished the can in two more swallows and handed the empty to Cade. At least he'd picked up a skill at all those stupid football parties his roommate, Ira, had dragged him to.

"Hell no, I don't mind. I just don't want to see you get hurt." Cade opened the trunk and set the beer inside along with the empties.

Eric opened the passenger door and got inside. He still wasn't sure what he'd say to Will. Guess he'd figure it out on the way down the mountain.

* * * *

Eric wiped his clammy hands on his jeans before knocking on the deep red painted door. It was almost midnight and he should probably turn around and run back to Cade, who was still waiting for him at the kerb.

After several moments, he knocked again before glancing over his shoulder. *Please don't make a fool of me, Will,* Eric prayed.

The door opened and Will, wearing nothing but a thin pair of sleep pants, blinked several times. "Eric?"

Eric was struck speechless while he took in the hard muscled body in front of him. *Oh my fucking God.* Before he could gather his thoughts, Will's attention turned to the car parked in front of his small house.

"Who's that?" Will asked.

"Cade, Becket's brother. He dropped me off," Eric stammered.

"Dropped you off from where?" Will's already deep voice had gone even lower.

"Can I talk to you?" When Will didn't answer immediately, Eric tried once more. "Please? I won't stay long, but I don't want to look like a fool in front of Cade."

Will took several steps back and pulled Eric into the house. "Wave goodbye," he instructed Eric.

Eric sent up a hand in thanks to Cade before closing the door. He turned to face Will and was met by a narrow-eyed gaze. "I'm sorry. Were you asleep?"

"It's after midnight on a work night, what do you think?" Will must've thought better of his gruff tone because his expression softened. He gestured to the deep sofa. "Have a seat."

Eric felt more than a little awkward as he sat down. It was obvious Will didn't want him there, and if the view of Will's magnificent body weren't so damn appealing, Eric probably would've left already.

"Now tell me what you were doing with that guy at this time of night." Will sat far enough away from Eric on the couch that they weren't touching and crossed his legs.

The movement drew Eric's attention to the hefty package tucked inside Will's pants. He pulled his gaze away and gathered his wits. The question was tricky. If he lied, and Will found out, things between them would be over before they got started, but he had no idea how Will would react to what Eric had to say. "We were talking," he swallowed, building up his courage, "and he was trying to teach me how to kiss."

Will's eyes narrowed to mere slits. "Why all the sudden do you need some stranger to teach you how to kiss?"

Eric scooted closer to Will. "Because I didn't want to make a fool of myself with you," he admitted. He tilted his chin up, hoping Will would take the hint.

In one smooth move, Will pulled Eric into his arms and kissed him. Unlike Cade, Will didn't start off gently, nor did he seek silent permission before thrusting his tongue into Eric's mouth.

Eric accepted the kiss gratefully and moved to straddle Will's lap. Within seconds, his body felt like it was on fire as Will's large hands began to squeeze Eric's ass. *Fuck.* The kiss was beyond anything Eric had expected. He began to move his hips, grinding his hardened cock against Will's abdomen. *More.* The realisation that he was close to getting everything he'd dreamed of hit him, and Eric decided to go for it. He pulled back enough to get his hand between their bodies, going all the way down to rest on Will's cock.

Will groaned into Eric's mouth as Eric wrapped his hand around the erection pressing against the thin cotton of Will's pants. It was yet another first for Eric as he rubbed the head of Will's cock with his thumb. He briefly wondered if he was doing it right, but Will's continued moans were answer enough.

Still battling Will's tongue with his own, Eric managed to unbutton the fly of Will's pyjamas and reach inside. A string of curse words sounded in Eric's mind as he touched another man's cock for the first time. Skin to skin, Will's dick was even more impressive, with thick veins and copious amounts of pre-cum leaking from the tip.

Will suddenly jerked his head back, breaking their kiss. "No," he said, shaking his head. He pushed Eric onto the sofa and stood before tucking his hard cock back into his pants. "I told you before, we can't do this, not yet."

Eric wiped his swollen lips. "Who's gonna know?" He stood and tried to worm his way back into Will's embrace, but Will held him at arm's length. "Please don't push me away."

"I know it doesn't seem like it, but I'm honestly doing this for both our sakes. It only takes one person to raise the question of what you were doing at my house after midnight to derail the entire investigation." Will slid his hands up from Eric's arms to cradle his face. "Go home, Eric."

"I don't wanna go," Eric said.

"I know, but the chemistry between us is like nothing I've ever experienced, and I can't have you around right now." Will leaned in and kissed Eric's forehead. "And for the record, I don't want you seeing that guy again. Either he's a really good teacher or you didn't need him in the first place, because that was one hell of a kiss."

Eric's body was still hyper-aware of each touch Will bestowed and when he was pulled into a hug, he could feel Will's erection pressing against him. "How long will I have to wait?"

"I don't know, but I promise I'll work my ass off to find the evidence we need to get that asshole behind bars."

Will's body felt so good to Eric that he didn't want to let go, so he continued the conversation, hoping to distract Will. "You know how some drugs get you addicted on the first try?"

"Yeah," Will answered.

"I think you're like that for me." Damn it, despite everything that had happened and everything that stood in their way, Eric was determined that Will would indeed be his first consensual lover. He bit his bottom lip. Earlier in the evening, he'd questioned whether it was possible to have a lasting relationship with his first, and now the answer seemed even more important to him than it had before.

"I'm sorry to hear that, because we're going to have to quit cold turkey, at least for a while longer." Will pulled back and walked to the front door. "I hate the thought of sending you out there on your own, is there someone you trust who can pick you up?"

Eric shook his head. "The only real friend I have is Becket, and I'm sure he's asleep by now."

Will rubbed the back of his neck. "I'd take you, but we can't take the chance of someone seeing me drop you off. Should I call a cab?"

"BK's only six blocks from here, I can walk it." Eric's chest tightened at the thought of being alone on the dark empty streets, but he didn't want to come off like a baby. "No problem," he assured Will.

Before Eric made it out the door, Will grabbed his upper arm. "Do us both a favour and try to stay away from me until this is over. I don't want to go through this again."

Whether Will meant it the way it sounded or not, all the hope and desire Eric had felt moments earlier turned sour in his gut. He stared at Will, but couldn't bring himself to agree with Will's decision. Without a word, he left Will's cute little bungalow and shut the door behind him.

With his head held high, Eric started back to BK House. He'd travelled two blocks when he heard a noise coming from a yard, dripping in dark shadows. Pausing, he stood as still as possible and waited for the noise to come again. After several moments, he turned and started to jog.

Although he didn't hear anything more, the tiny hairs on the back of his neck continued to stand on end. For some reason he couldn't shake the feeling that he was being watched. The last block was taken at an all-out run, and by the time he dug into his pocket for the key to the front door, he was out of breath and out of sorts.

The last thing he wanted was to spend the rest of his life afraid of the fucking dark.

Chapter Three

Will walked into the police station almost an hour late for work. He couldn't blame Eric for oversleeping, because despite what he'd said to Eric the previous evening, he hadn't been able to relax enough to do anything but lie in bed and stare at the ceiling. His restlessness was worse after the late-night visit and subsequent kiss and bump-and-grind session with Eric.

"James! Get in here," Captain Vince Prater yelled before Will could sit down.

"Shit," Will mumbled under his breath. Rarely did his captain speak with him directly, so being called into the office couldn't be good. Was it possible someone saw Cade drop Eric off at his house? With a groan, Will prepared himself for the ass chewing that would surely be the result of such an offense.

He entered the office and stood just inside the door. "Yes, sir?"

"Shut the door," Prater ordered.

The fact that he hadn't been asked to take a seat was another bad sign. Will did as instructed and leaned against the closed door.

"Byron Long doesn't seem to be too happy with the way things went yesterday," Vince began.

"Nor should he be." Will refused to make excuses, but no way would he take the blame. "You were the one who pulled me off because you felt I was wasting time on an open-and-shut case."

Captain Prater ran a finger over his short grey moustache. "Byron told me the physical evidence was enough to convict. As you are aware, this department has suffered the same budget cuts as every other department in the city. My job is to make sure we run efficiently, but if you'd had an objection to my orders, you should've stated them at the time."

"I value your orders, and I'm not in the habit of arguing with my superiors, sir." It was a game, and Will knew it, worse, he'd become fairly adept at playing it. Vince needed to distance himself from the fuck-up and it seemed Will would end up taking the heat if he didn't come up with something to give Byron. "But if you'd like me to continue to look into the case, I'd definitely be willing."

"No overtime on this one, James," Vince warned.

Will nodded in understanding. "I'll get started right away."

Will left the captain's office and stopped by the coffee pot on his way to his desk. The sludge matched his mood perfectly and he poured himself a big cup. Sitting at his desk, he powered up his computer and waited for the ancient piece of equipment to come to life.

Despite what the captain had ordered, there was no way to gather the needed evidence in the span of a normal workday, especially because he knew he'd have to travel to Loveland, Colorado if he really wanted to start at the beginning.

Before he was known as Jigger, Paul Williams had spent the first eighteen years of his life in the same city, and although Jigger's parents were no longer alive, Jigger had surely left some kind of trail there.

Will took a sip of coffee before looking through public housing records, searching for neighbours that might still be in the area. If he got lucky, he might be able to conduct an interview over the phone.

It didn't take long to get exasperated. Although the Williams family had lived in the same house for years, most of the neighbourhood they called home consisted of apartments and rental houses. Shit. The search wouldn't be as easy as he'd hoped, but he was determined to talk to someone, anyone, who remembered Paul Williams.

* * * *

With a bottle of Wild Turkey tucked discreetly under his jacket, Eric made his way into the house and up the stairs to his room. He opened the door and was glad to see the room empty for a change.

Yes!

Although he'd never said a word, it was obvious Rusty didn't approve of Eric's new drinking habit. *Too bad*, Eric thought. *I'm not hurting anyone.* One way or another, he always managed to get his homework finished, and he never missed a class, so what was the problem?

Eric kicked off his shoes and grabbed his laptop, keeping the bottle of whisky at his side. He pulled up his favourite porn site and unscrewed the top of the bottle. It had been three days since the kiss with Will, and Eric's sex drive was working overtime.

He unzipped his jeans before pushing them, along with his underwear, down to mid-thigh, leaving his flaccid cock exposed. He started scanning the newest uploaded videos, looking for something in particular.

"Gotcha," he said, clicking on a video link of one man giving another head. He set the laptop between his spread legs and wrapped his hand around his cock. With a firm grip, he started to jerk himself off, stopping only long enough to open the bottle of whisky and take a swallow.

Since touching Will's cock, Eric had jerked off at least four times a day. He hadn't been kidding when he'd told Will he was addicted. There were times he thought he'd wear his dick out before he even had a chance to use it properly.

Thirty minutes, a third of a bottle of Wild Turkey and two orgasms later, Eric was definitely feeling better. He was drifting in a satisfied haze when the doorknob turned back and forth several times.

"Eric?" Rusty called through the closed door.

"Shit," Eric grumbled and stuffed his cum rag under the mattress. He got to his feet and pulled up his pants before shutting the laptop. The biggest downfall of having a roommate was the inability to fully enjoy the afterglow.

By the time he opened the door, Rusty's brow had furrowed, or did his roommate's look of disdain have more to do with the bottle in his hand? "Sorry 'bout that," Eric apologised.

Rusty, all one hundred and ten pounds of him, stomped into the room and set his books on his desk. "It stinks in here."

Eric was growing fond of the smell of cum, whisky and sweat, but he knew not everyone shared his opinion. "I'll go find some air freshener," he offered.

"Don't bother, I have my own." Rusty pulled open a drawer and removed a large can of disinfecting spray.

Great. Instead of smelling like a guy's room, the place would reek of hospital sterilisation. Eric waved his arms, warding off the cloud of mist Rusty shot his way. "Dude!"

Rusty shrugged and replaced the can before shutting his drawer. "I need to study."

"It's Friday night," Eric reminded him.

Rusty rolled his eyes. "How you can fully enjoy your weekend without getting your classwork out of the way first is beyond me."

Eric set his laptop on his desk before flopping onto the bed. "You didn't happen to see Becket downstairs, did ya?"

"He was at dinner." Rusty didn't even bother to look up from his textbook. "Jack made fried chicken." He finally glanced at Eric. "It was good, but I see you drank your dinner instead." He gave a dramatic sigh before mumbling, "Again."

"You know, maybe if you weren't such an uptight asshole and actually took a drink now and then, you'd have friends to spend your time with instead of studying all the time," Eric quipped.

"Yeah, because that drinking thing is working out so well. You have what, one friend and you don't even know where he is? Sure, I want to be just like you." Rusty slammed his book shut and stood. "I think I'll go see if one of the study rooms is empty."

Eric set the bottle on the desk, which also doubled as a nightstand, and closed his eyes as the door slammed shut. "Prick," he grumbled.

Even though he'd said it, in his heart, Eric knew Rusty was a good kid. Moreover, he knew his newly acquired lifestyle had more to do with the trial and his desire for Will than the need to get drunk every night.

He just felt so damn lonely all the time, which he knew was no one's fault but his own. Why did he have to be stuck on Will? Why couldn't he be like every other college student and go after anything that had two legs?

Mind made up, Eric reached for his phone and scrolled through his contacts before hitting the one person he really needed to talk to.

"Hey," Will answered. "Everything okay?"

"Not really. I wondered if you'd meet me somewhere, a place where no one will see us together?" Eric held his breath, waiting for Will's answer.

"I'd be tempted if I was in town, but I'm in Colorado."

"You went on vacation?" Eric couldn't believe Will would just take off like that.

"I wish. No, I'm hunting down some old neighbours of Jigger's. On my own dime, I might add, so I'd better have more luck than I did today."

It didn't seem to matter what Will talking about, the effect his voice had on Eric was predictable. Eric reached down and adjusted his cock. "Wanna have phone sex?"

Will chuckled. "Have you ever had phone sex before?"

"Hell no," Eric admitted. "I've never had sex while being conscious before, but I've been watching a bunch of porn lately, and I'm sure once you're ready…" He let his voice trail off before making too big a fool of himself.

"Porn's fun to watch at times, but not always true to the way things really are."

"Really? What's different?" Eric upended his bottle of whisky as he waited for the answer. He had to admit that he enjoyed Will's exasperated sigh.

"Well, for one thing, after you come, it takes more than a couple of minutes to recover before going at it again."

Eric thought of his two earlier orgasms, but decided not to mention it. He took another drink. "And?"

"Are you drinking?" Will asked.

Caught with his hand in the cookie jar, Eric set the bottle on the desk. "Not right now."

"But you have been, right?"

"It's Friday night," Eric reminded Will. "Half the kids on campus are drinking."

"Yeah, and I don't give a shit about them, I care about what you do because I like you, and getting drunk alone in your room is..."

"Pathetic," Eric finished for him.

"No, dangerous."

"How am I putting myself in danger?" Eric questioned.

"Drunk people don't make wise decisions."

Eric started to wonder whether dating an older man was what he really wanted to do. "I don't need a stand-in father, Will. I called because I missed you."

"I'm not trying to sound like your dad, but I've been a cop for a long time, and I've seen what too much alcohol can do." Will huffed out a long breath. "Damn it, Eric, I *care* what happens to you."

Eric bit his tongue. He wanted to argue, but he recognised that the rage simmering inside him had nothing to do with Will's warning and everything to do with the overwhelming feeling of helplessness that threatened to drown him each day. The whisky helped, but unless he drank enough to pass out it never really helped enough to get through the night without waking in a cold sweat.

"Eric?" Will prompted.

"Have you found anything at all?" Eric asked.

"An older woman who remembered Pauly—her name for him, not mine—from his old neighbourhood. She said he was a nice boy who tended to be gullible. I guess he hung out with the older kids and they usually talked him into doing their dirty work for them, but according to her, he had a big heart when the other boys weren't around. Unfortunately, a statement like that would go a long way in explaining to a jury how Jigger was caught driving a stolen car when he was still a senior in high school."

"So he was a good kid who also got into trouble. What does that prove?" Eric refused to see any positive qualities in the man who had drugged and raped him. "Maybe you'll get lucky and run into his kindergarten teacher."

"Watch it," Will growled. "I know you're upset, but I've spent a hell of a lot of my own goddamn money to come out here."

Eric squeezed his eyes shut and rolled to his side. He hugged his legs against his chest and clutched the phone in his hand. "Sorry. I wish I could blame the Wild Turkey, but I think it's a lot more than that."

"Understandable," Will said. "But you'll have to learn to trust me if you're serious about seeing me after all this is done."

"Trust is a hard thing for me to come by these days, but I'll try," Eric confessed.

"In the meantime, please do me a favour and stop drinking."

"Only if you promise to call me when you get back to town."

"I'll be home by Sunday afternoon."

"So you'll meet me?" Eric asked.

"We'll see."

* * * *

After his talk with Will, Eric felt like shit for running Rusty out of the room. He was on his way to find his roommate when Becket met him in the hall.

"Hey, I was wondering if you were around," Becket said.

"I've been in my room."

Becket waved his hand in front of his face. "Drinking, I gather."

Eric shrugged. "What's up?"

"I thought maybe you'd feel like going to a late movie. Locky was supposed to take me to see the new Batman, but he's tied up with some freshman drama that's going on downstairs, so he suggested I ask you."

Eric had never been much of a Batman fan, but he did understand the appeal of Christian Bale. "Give me five minutes, and I'll meet you downstairs."

"Cool."

Eric ran back into his room and put on one of his favourite old T-shirts, and slipped his feet into a pair of sneakers. His gaze landed on the bottle of whisky and he stopped long enough to put the cap back on and hide it in the back of his closet before grabbing his wallet and keys.

He made it downstairs with a minute to spare and looked around for Becket. He eventually found him in the large rec room, talking to Chase. "What's going on?"

Becket and Chase both looked over their shoulder to one of the study rooms. "Charlie and Locky pulled Rusty in there for some kind of meeting or something and he just went nuts, screaming and shit. I don't know what it's about, but it must be serious."

Guilt settled heavily in Eric's gut. "He got mad at me earlier for drinking in the room," he admitted.

Becket shook his head. "No, I don't think it was something as simple as that. Locky and I were up *taking a nap* when Charlie called him downstairs. I think it has something to do with his parents."

"Should we get one of his friends or something?" Eric asked.

Chase and Becket looked at each other, but it was Chase who answered. "I've never seen him hang around anyone in particular."

"Come on, he's gotta have *someone* he talks to," Eric argued.

"Professor Ryan, but he's Rusty's advisor. I don't know if they talk about anything but school. Hell, I don't know if Rusty *ever* talks about anything but math and science." Becket turned towards the door. "If we're going to make the movie, we should leave. Chase's coming with us, too."

Although Eric wasn't close to Rusty, he couldn't just leave him without trying to do something to help. "Ya know what, you guys go ahead. I think I'll hang back and see if Rusty needs anything."

Chase whistled. "Giving up Christian Bale for Rusty? I'm impressed."

In an unexpected move, Becket wrapped his arm around Eric's shoulders and gave him a squeeze. "So am I."

Eric remembered the way Rusty had given him the space he needed after the mistrial and had never once asked him questions about what had happened. He shrugged and pulled away from Becket. "I'm his roommate. It's the right thing to do."

"Yeah," Becket agreed. "Catch up with you tomorrow?"

"Sure." Eric waited for Becket and Chase to leave before approaching the closed door. He knocked softly and waited.

Locky opened the door far enough to stick his head out. "Yes?"

"Is there anything I can do?" Eric asked.

Locky held up a finger. "Just a sec." He looked over his shoulder and spoke to the others in the room with him before slipping out to join Eric. "Unfortunately, I don't think anything can really be done to help Rusty right now. His parents were killed in a car accident earlier this evening."

Eric regretted that he'd never tried to get to know Rusty better than a casual greeting here and there. "But, we were just upstairs and he didn't say anything about it."

"He didn't know. The police felt it would be better to pass the information along to Rusty in person, so they called Charlie."

Eric tried to think of a way to help his new roommate. "Chase told me that Rusty talks to Professor Ryan a lot. Do you think I should try to call *him*?"

Locky glanced back to the closed door. "I don't know…maybe. Right now he's barely talking to anyone." He rubbed his stubbled chin. "Let me ask him."

While Locky ducked back into the room to talk to Rusty, Eric grabbed the campus directory off the long table most guys used to study or play games. He did a quick search for Professor Ryan, but came up short. Under the Science Department listings, he found Professor Adam Ryan's name and his office number, but no mention of a phone number outside of the campus.

Locky rejoined Eric and shook his head. "Rusty said Ryan doesn't have a phone, but he can usually be found in the lab."

"At this time of night?" Eric questioned. Was it possible that Rusty had met his match in the geek department? "Does he know where Professor Ryan lives?"

Locky lifted his shoulders. "All he said was that he'd probably be in his lab working with Professor Corto Delgado."

Eric blew out a frustrated breath. "Okay. I'll run over to the science building and see if I can find him."

"Thanks," Locky said. "Mention of the professor's name was the first sign of life Rusty's exhibited since he tore the room up."

* * * *

Eric jogged halfway to the science building before slowing to a walk. Damn, he shouldn't have drunk so much. He was almost to the liberal arts building when he heard a noise off to his left, which wasn't altogether unusual for a college campus, so he didn't pay it much attention.

It wasn't until the steady sound of footsteps seemed to keep with Eric's pace and direction that he became concerned. He stared into the surrounding area, poorly lit by small pools of overhead lights, and called out. "Who's there?"

After several seconds, a man's voice came from the shadows, and Eric's breath froze in his lungs.

"I need to talk to you."

With his hands curled into fists, Eric shook his head. "Stay away from me!"

Eric didn't give Jigger a chance to come any closer. Despite his earlier fatigue, adrenaline fuelled him into a fast sprint towards his destination. *Please be open. Please be open*, he silently prayed as he raced to the brick building.

Running up the steps, Eric's hand closed around the old brass handle and yanked. He almost cried when the door opened immediately. A security guard, sitting right inside the building, jumped to his feet in surprise.

"The...man who...raped me...is out there," Eric said between pants. He leaned against the wall and bent over to rest his hands on his knees, trying to keep from falling to the floor. "Call the police."

The guard jumped into action. He grabbed his cell phone and called campus security as he rushed out of the building. Eric pulled out his own phone and called Will.

"I thought you'd be asleep by now," Will answered.

Still breathing heavily, Eric gave into his body's demands and slid down the wall to the floor. "Rusty's parents died, so I was going across campus to get Professor Ryan and I heard a noise, but it wasn't just any noise because next thing I know I hear Jigger's voice saying he needed to talk to me. I ran to the science building and the guard is outside trying to find him," he quickly relayed, barely taking a breath between sentences.

"How close was he?" Will asked, his voice taking on a gravelly quality.

"I don't know. What's that have to do with anything?"

"Because he's been ordered to stay at least five hundred feet away from you. It's the first thing the cops will ask."

Eric wiped the sweat from his forehead. "Well, excuse me for not having a fucking measuring tape with me. All I know is he's out there."

"Shit," Will swore. "Okay, the most important thing is that you're safe. Just make sure you don't leave that building without an escort. Hopefully, the police will find Jigger and haul him in."

"Then what?" Eric asked.

"You'll have to go to the station and file a report. I'll call a buddy of mine and see if he'll go in. Once you get there, ask for Detective Riggs."

Eric suddenly remembered the reason he'd crossed the campus in the first place. "Okay, but first I need to go upstairs and find Professor Ryan."

"Do not leave that building without an escort, do you hear me?"

Unlike Will's earlier warning, Eric could feel the protective quality in Will's words. "Don't worry about that. No way I'm going back out there without someone with a gun standing beside me."

"Eric," Will said after a few moments of silence. "I wish I was there for you."

The corners of Eric's mouth turned up in a slight smile. "Yeah, I wish you were, too, but I know what you're doing is important."

"We're going to get this guy put away for a long time, just have faith."

"I do. In you," Eric added.

* * * *

It took Eric several minutes to find the lab Professor Ryan shared with Professor Corto Delgado, but he eventually came to the heavy steel door with both men's names on it. He pounded his fist against the cold metal, hoping Professor Ryan was really working and not at home.

Eric knocked twice more before turning to leave. He'd only walked a few steps when the door opened.

"Yes?" a man asked, sticking his head out the door.

"Professor Ryan?" Eric asked. He'd never met the advanced microbiology professor, but the man looked absolutely nothing like the professors he had in the engineering department.

Dressed in a faded pair of jeans and tight white T-shirt, Professor Ryan's short brown hair was spiked in odd angles as if he'd just woken up. "Yes. Can I help you?"

"My name's Eric? I live over at the BK House?" Eric had no idea why he was suddenly speaking in questions. Maybe it was the sexy dishevelled teacher staring at him. "Rusty Bonham's parents were both killed in an accident earlier this evening and you're the only person he seems to want to talk to."

Professor Ryan's expression clouded, making it impossible for Eric to read him. Eric decided to try again. "Is there any way you could go back with me to BK and talk to him, maybe help him through the shock?"

"Yes, of course. One moment, please." Professor Ryan went back into the lab and closed the door.

Eric shoved his hands in his pockets and leaned against the wall, wondering how long he was supposed to wait. He had his own problems to deal with, but the longer he remained inside, the more likely campus security would apprehend Jigger.

The door opened once again and Professor Ryan stepped into the hall. He'd traded in his white lab coat for a battered denim jacket. "Sorry. I had to fill Manuel in on what's happened."

Manuel? Although Eric had never heard the name, he assumed it must belong to Professor Corto Delgado. That whole two-surname thing had always fucked with Eric's head. As they walked to the stairs, Eric felt it was only right to let the professor in on what else was going on.

"I don't know if Rusty's told you anything about me, but I was raped before the semester began."

Professor Ryan nodded. "He's mentioned it."

"Yeah, I figured." Eric hated the fact that his rape was still something people around campus talked about. "Anyway, on my way over, the man accused of raping me was following me. Right now the campus police are trying to find him."

Professor Ryan stopped walking. "So he's likely still out there?"

Eric nodded.

"Hang on a minute." Professor Ryan ran back to the lab and swiped his identification card. The door opened and he disappeared inside once more.

When the door opened again, Professor Ryan was closely followed by an incredibly hot Spanish guy. *Manuel Corto Delgado.* Eric let the sexy name wash through him as he took a moment to fantasise about the visiting professor.

"Manuel is better equipped to deal with your attacker, should the need arise," Professor Ryan announced.

No shit. Professor Corto Delgado definitely had a lethal look to him. Although his muscles weren't huge, they were definitely prominent underneath his dress shirt, which Eric happened to notice was buttoned all wrong.

Professor Corto Delgado simply nodded in agreement and followed them closely down the hall.

Eric glanced over his shoulder as they made it to the front doors. He wasn't sure if the Spaniard spoke English or not. "After we get back to BK House, I need to go to the local police station to fill out a complaint against Jigger. Would you mind taking me?"

Professor Corto Delgado lifted a single black eyebrow at the question. "Then perhaps it would be better to drive." Without another word, he veered left down a long hallway towards the faculty parking lot.

Eric glanced at Professor Ryan. "Do you think he minds, Professor Ryan?" he whispered.

Professor Ryan grinned. "Naw, Manny love's playing the white knight, and you're not my student, so feel free to call me Adam."

"And I'm Manuel," Professor Corto Delgado announced, leading the way to a shiny black Lexus LS.

Manuel opened the rear passenger-side door for Eric before opening the front passenger door for Adam. "You'll have to give me directions," he mentioned as he slid in behind the steering wheel.

Eric ran his palm over the soft white leather seats. "I'm in love with this car," he admitted.

Manuel laughed. "So is Adam. He's the one who helped pick it out."

Kudos to Adam for having excellent taste. The car had to've cost close to a hundred grand. Eric tore his gaze away from all the gadgets in the backseat when they pulled out of the parking lot.

"Just take a right and then your first left." Although BK House wasn't officially on campus, it was only half a block away. "Right there," Eric said when they got close.

Manuel pulled into an available slot and turned off the engine. "I will wait for you here," he told Eric.

"Thanks." Eric got out and shut the door. He waited for Adam who seemed to be in deep conversation with Manuel for several minutes.

Eventually, Adam leant over and gave Manuel a kiss, surprising the hell out of Eric. When Adam joined Eric he shrugged. "I figured since you live here you're used to seeing two men kiss."

"I am, but I've never watched two professors kiss." Eric led Adam up the front steps to the door. Before opening it, he grinned at Adam. "You have very good taste though."

Adam chuckled. "Yeah," he agreed.

Chapter Four

It was almost three o'clock in the morning when Manuel parked in front of BK House. "Would you mind telling Adam I'm out here?"

Eric was so physically and emotionally drained by the night's activities, he barely had the energy to answer. "No problem." He started to get out but stopped and glanced back at Manuel. "You didn't have to stay with me at the station all night, but I'm thankful you did."

"Think nothing of it. It was the right thing to do."

With a weary sigh, Eric got out of the car and climbed up the steps. He found Rusty asleep on the rec room sofa and Adam sitting across from him, head tilted back, eyes closed. Eric reached out and touched Adam's shoulder.

Adam's dark brown eyes sprang open and he immediately sat straight up in his chair, his focus squarely on a still-sleeping Rusty. After several moments, he lifted his head to look at Eric. "How did it go?"

"Not good, but I'm sure Manuel will fill you in." Eric gestured to Rusty. "How's he doing?"

Adam returned his attention to Rusty. "Not well, I'm afraid. He finally settled down enough to sleep about an hour ago."

"Manuel's waiting for you out front."

Adam's expression appeared torn. "I hate to leave him like this."

"He'll be okay." Eric dropped into one of the recliners. "I'll sleep down here in case he wakes up."

Adam smiled at Eric. "You've proven yourself to be a good friend."

Eric shook his head. "No, I haven't, at least not yet."

Before he left, Adam moved to stand over Rusty. He reached down and drew a gentle hand down Rusty's cheek. Turning back to Eric, he pointed towards the slip of paper on the coffee table. "I wrote down Manuel's phone number. Please ask Rusty to call when he wakes up."

"Will do." After Adam left, Eric dug his phone out of his pocket and turned it on for the first time since arriving at the police station. He knew Will had left several messages because he'd eventually called Detective Riggs to find out what was going on.

Despite the hour, Eric called Will as he'd promised to do once he returned home.

Will spoke into the phone, but his speech was so garbled with sleep that Eric couldn't understand him. He suddenly felt bad for waking Will. "Go back to sleep. I'll call you later," Eric told him.

"I'm awake," Will said, still groggy. "I'm sorry, I didn't mean to fall asleep."

"Don't be. Believe me, I'll probably sleep most of the day once I finally get to bed."

"Anything new happen after the last time I called Riggs?" Will asked.

"You mean besides the fact that they all think I'm delusional?"

The cops had located Jigger easily enough. He'd been at his apartment, entertaining some twink. It was still hard for Eric to believe that anyone would willingly let an accused rapist fuck them. The whole thing made his skin crawl. "I'm not crazy," Eric added. "I know it had to have been him."

"I don't think you're crazy, but since you didn't actually see his face, there isn't much that can be done. The important thing is that you're safe."

Funny, Eric didn't feel very safe. The campus was his turf, not Jigger's. It was the one place, besides BK, that he should be able to walk around without fear of being attacked. He stifled a yawn. "Anyway," he began, refusing to comment on Will's statement. "I can't seem to keep my eyes open, so I'll talk to you later."

"I'll call you tomorrow when I get in," Will said.

"Okay." Eric hung up and shoved the phone back into his pocket. He felt eyes on him and looked up to find Rusty staring at him. Without his usual wire-frame glasses, Rusty was actually kind of cute. "Hey."

"Did Professor Ryan leave?"

Eric nodded. "Just a few minutes ago." He gestured to the piece of paper on the table. "He left Manu — Professor Corto Delgado's number. He said you should give him a call later if you feel like it."

Rusty pushed himself up into a sitting position and rubbed the back of his neck. "I should've known better than to fall asleep on the couch." He got to his feet. "You going up?"

"Yeah." Eric went to stand by Rusty. "You can lean on me if you need to."

Rusty looked up at Eric. "Why're you being so nice to me?"

"I should've been all along. Sorry for being a dick earlier. I'm just dealing with a lot of shit right now."

"I know."

Once they reached the room, Eric kicked off his sneakers, turned off the light and fell into bed. "I'm sorry about your folks," he said as his eyelids drifted closed.

"Thanks, sadly it wasn't all that unexpected," Rusty said before a soft snore sounded from his side of the room.

Eric wondered what he meant, but before he could think too hard about it, he, too, fell asleep.

* * * *

"Are you sure you don't need me to go with you?" Eric asked. He'd spent the previous day napping and hanging out in the room with Rusty, but it was time for his roommate to head back to his hometown of Ruttland, Vermont. As much as Eric wanted to be there for Rusty, there was no way he could afford the plane ticket, but he'd beg, borrow or steal if his newest friend needed him.

"Thanks for offering, but it's something I'd rather do alone." Rusty carried his small suitcase down the staircase.

Locky, with Becket at his side, came into the living room from outside. "All set?"

Rusty nodded, handing his suitcase to Locky. "Thanks."

"No problem. We'll wait for you in the car," Locky said.

Rusty turned back to Eric and gave him a tentative smile. "I'll be back next weekend."

"You have my number, so call if you need to talk or anything," Eric reminded him.

Tears filled Rusty's eyes. "I've never had a friend."

"Bullshit," Eric said, rolling his eyes. Rusty might be quirky, but Eric had quickly discovered what an overall nice guy he was.

Rusty shook his head, and took his heavy backpack from Eric. "I'm not kidding, but I like that you think I am."

Eric walked Rusty out before going back inside and upstairs. He did a bit of studying and even tried watching porn, but nothing held his attention. Now that he had the room to himself, he discovered it wasn't as much fun as he thought it'd be.

With one eye on the clock, he practically jumped on the phone when it finally rang. "Hey," he greeted Will.

"Sorry I'm later than I thought I'd be, but I think you'll like the reason."

"Does it involve me getting to see you?" Eric asked.

"As a matter of fact it does, but I need you to do me a favour," Will said.

"Okaaayy," Eric warily agreed.

"Do you have money for a taxi?"

"Not really, but Becket's upstairs. He'll take me anywhere I need to go, and since he kinda knows I like you, he won't tell anyone."

Will was quiet for several moments before continuing. "I stopped by Mom and Dad's on the way home and Dad got on my case because I haven't been to Sunday dinner in months, so he won't let me leave."

"Oh." Eric was afraid he knew where Will was going.

"The good news is that Mom invited you for dinner. Soooo, I was hoping you'd come."

Eric stared up at the ceiling. He hadn't even officially started dating Will and he was expected to meet his parents? "I don't know. Don't you think it'd be better to wait until we know each other better?"

"No. Actually, I thought it was a perfect idea. My parents are amazing, and I want to talk to my dad about the case. I think he might have some interesting insights."

"Why? Is he a lawyer?" Eric realised he knew very little about Will's family.

"No, he's worked maintenance at the courthouse since he got out of high school nearly thirty-seven years ago. Don't let his job fool ya though, my dad's the smartest man I've ever met."

It warmed Eric's heart to hear Will speak of his dad with such high regard. He still didn't want to go, but the fact that it seemed so important to Will helped sway him. "Okay," he eventually agreed.

"Great. They live at fifteen-oh-four Benson Mills Drive."

Eric found an old McDonalds receipt on his desk and wrote the address on the back. "Okay. When?"

"As soon as you can get here." Will cleared his throat. "I'm looking forward to seeing you."

"Me, too."

* * * *

By the time Will hung up the phone, he was grinning from ear to ear. He walked into the living room and sat on the sofa. "Eric'll be here as soon as he gets a ride."

"You should've picked him up," his dad, Henry, grumbled.

"You know I can't be seen with him yet. Hell, I shouldn't see him now, but I can't help myself."

"First of all, you may be thirty-six, but you know better than to use that language in your mother's house, and secondly, you can't continue to sneak around with that young man."

Will opened his mouth to protest, but his dad shot him that father look that shut him up.

"I didn't say you shouldn't see him or that you should go the opposite way and take him out on the town, but if you treat whatever's going on between the two of you like it's something to be ashamed of, one or both of you will start to believe it." Henry shook his head. "I'd hate to see that happen. This is the first date you've brought home in years, and I'll admit, it's nice to see that twinkle in your eyes again."

"Thanks, Dad, but if the defence finds out…"

"Worry about the jury, not the lawyers. Give the jury something to hold onto besides the fact that you may or may not be involved with the victim."

"I could lose my job," Will reminded his dad.

"Sure, and if your feelings for Eric are just casual, I would warn you against it, but I think this young man is different."

"You haven't even met him." There were times when Will wished his parents didn't take such an interest in his love life. This was one of them.

"No, I haven't formally met him, but I've watched him sit outside the courtroom day after day. I even talked to him on several occasions." Henry held his hand up before Will could object. "He didn't know who I was, and at the time, I didn't know you were interested in him, so don't tell me I was meddling."

"Fine. What did the two of you talk about?" Will asked, suddenly curious.

Henry scratched the top of his head, a habit he'd had for years. It was a wonder he had any hair left. "Nothing of importance, really. It wasn't what he said, but how he said it that impressed me."

"Yeah, I guess he's pretty smart."

Henry grinned. "It wasn't his intelligence I was impressed by. Do you have any idea how many people who come through that courthouse on a daily basis pretend to not even see me? It's a rare occurrence when someone even looks me in the eyes and smiles, let alone takes the time to talk to me." His grin grew into a smile. "But Eric did. He was either sitting on that bench or pacing back and forth, worried about what was going on inside, but he actually took the time to ask me each and every day that I saw him how I was doing, and it wasn't idle chitchat. I could tell he really wanted to know the answer. That's something special. That's the kind of man you deserve."

A strange sense of pride filled Will. Why, he probably couldn't put into words, but it was nice to know he was finally attracted to a nice guy. "I've always felt proud that you worked at the courthouse," he admitted.

Of course there had been kids growing up who made comments about Will's dad being a janitor, but he'd never let narrow minds get to him. He'd gone with his dad to work enough over the years, so he knew exactly how hard his dad worked and how important his job was in maintaining the gorgeous old building.

"Thanks," his dad said. "I know it's not the kind of job most people aspire to have, but it's good, honest work and it's allowed me to take care of my family."

"It sure has." Will had never really wanted for anything growing up, but then he'd never really asked for anything. The day after making the freshman football team, a new ball and set of cleats were waiting for him in his room when he got home from school. It was like his mom and dad had always known what he needed and provided it if it was necessary and affordable. It bred a sense of comfort and trust in his parents that Will knew most kids didn't have, and he would be forever grateful for the way they'd accepted him completely when he'd come out to them. It had taken his older brother a little longer to come around, but to be fair, Stan was a senior in high school when, as a junior, Will came out to first his family then his friends. It hadn't taken long before the entire student body knew he preferred dicks over chicks.

Nowadays, Stan was cool with Will's lifestyle and lived in Seattle with his girlfriend of four years. Despite their mother's desire for grandchildren, Stan refused to get married until he felt the time was right.

When the doorbell rang, Will jumped up and wiped his hands on his jeans. "I've already told you about Eric's folks, so don't ask him about them, okay?"

"They're not even worth discussing," his dad told him.

"Good. Okay." Will couldn't believe how nervous he was. Strangely, it wasn't Eric meeting his parents that made him feel weird, it was his desire to pull Eric into his arms that was different. More than one ex-boyfriend had claimed that Will was too standoffish and cold, something he'd never denied. He'd learned with his first love to protect his heart until he knew for sure he could trust the person he was dating. Although he didn't know Eric as well as he hoped to in the future, he felt different when Eric was around, more relaxed and definitely more sexually attracted than he'd been with anyone in years.

Will opened the door and smiled at Eric. Before stepping back to allow him entrance, he took a moment to wave to Becket. "I'm glad you came." He ushered Eric into the house. "Come in."

Eric entered the home and shut the door. "I'm still having a hard time understanding why you invited me."

With only a moment's hesitation, Will pulled Eric into his arms. "You'd have to meet them soon or later, they're a big part of my life."

Eric looked surprised at the comment.

Everything his dad said ran on a loop through Will's mind. Eric was still new to being out of the closet, and asking him to hide his feelings had been wrong. Will moved Eric closer to the staircase, out of his father's view, and leant down to kiss him.

It only took a moment for Eric to reciprocate and soon the two were pressed so close there was no doubt how aroused they both were. Will lapped at Eric's mouth, growing hornier by the second. With each lash of Eric's tongue against his, Will wanted to toss Eric over his shoulder and carry him upstairs to his old boyhood room.

It was his father's voice that splashed a bucket of cold water on their interlude. "Are you two gonna stand by the stairs kissing all evening or are we going to eat?"

Will broke the kiss and rested his forehead against Eric's. Without breaking contact, he answered, "Be right there."

Eric's complexion turned bright red as he reached between them. He rubbed the front of Will's jeans and shook his head. "You'd better stop that or you're going to embarrass us even more."

"No way in hell I can stop it with you touching me like that," he whispered.

With an audible sigh, Eric stepped back, breaking all physical contact. "Let's talk about something else. How was your trip?"

"Long, but I think I have a better idea of the kind of man Jigger has become." Will was thankful that talk of Jigger helped slowly deflate his erection. "There's something else I found out. Jigger used to live in Houma, Louisiana before moving here to work as a bartender for Fallon's on Fifth."

Eric shook his head. "So?"

"Fallon Barrett lived thirty-some odd miles from Houma. Now according to Fallon, he didn't know Jigger before he hired him, but I find it strange that they lived that close to each other and both ended up here at the same time."

Eric furrowed his brow before nodding. "I see what you mean."

"Dinner's ready," Will's mother called from the kitchen.

"I don't think they're interested in eating," Will's dad answered.

"We're coming," Will called. "Come on before Dad really starts laying on the guilt."

* * * *

Eric accepted the large bowl of mashed potatoes. "It all looks delicious. Thanks for inviting me."

"It's our pleasure," Violet, Will's mother, said.

Eric had been pleasantly surprised to find the nice older man from the courthouse when he entered the living room. It had gone a long way to putting him at ease, and soon he felt truly welcome in the James' home.

"So tell me about your studies," Henry began. "What do you plan to do once you get your engineering degree?"

Eric pushed his spoon down into the centre of the mashed potatoes, making a well for his gravy. "Civil engineering is what I'm concentrating on. I like the thought of planning infrastructure and stuff."

"It's an honourable profession," Violet said, adding another piece of barbeque chicken to Eric's plate.

Will snorted and nearly choked on his iced tea. "Sorry." He wiped his mouth and nose on a freshly pressed napkin. He flashed Eric a dazzling smile. "I was holding out for a doctor, but they seem harder to come by than I thought."

Henry reached over and flicked Will on the side of the head with his finger. "Watch it."

Wincing, Will rubbed the side of his head. It was obvious to Eric that it was a familiar form of punishment. "Sorry, Mom," Will apologised.

Eric bit the inside of his cheek to keep from laughing. It was a completely different side to the normally gruff detective, and Eric found himself completely falling for the son of Henry and Violet.

* * * *

After dinner, Will helped his mom with the dishes before giving her a kiss on the cheek. "It was great, as usual. Thanks for being so welcoming to Eric."

"I like him. I can't understand how a mother could turn her back on him," his mom said.

"Me either, but he seems to be adjusting. I don't think they were close to begin with, which hopefully will make the transition easier for him." Will hung the dishcloth on the handle of the stove. "We're gonna take off."

"Keep him safe," his mom reminded.

"Always." Will left the kitchen in search of his dad and Eric. He found them in the garage drinking beer.

Eric looked guilty as Will took in the scene, but Will decided to let Eric off the hook. "You know, this is the only room of the house my mom allows alcohol," he told Eric.

Eric brightened. "Yeah, that's what your dad said."

Will looked around the large two-car garage. Although one bay held his mom's small sedan, his dad opted to park his truck outside so he could use his half for a makeshift man cave. The space had been kept relatively the same since Will was a kid with the exception of the couch. About every six or seven years, his mom ordered a new sofa for the living room and the old one always managed to wind up in the garage. The old green vinyl recliner was the same, but Will doubted his dad would ever part with the damn thing.

"Ready to go?" Will asked.

Eric sat up a little straighter. "Oh, sure, let me call Becket."

"No need. I'll give ya a ride." Will hoped to give Eric the ride of his life once they got back to his place, but he didn't want to push.

Eric finished his beer before going straight to the recycling bin and tossing it in, leading Will to the assumption that it wasn't his first. "Thank you for a great evening, Mr James."

Will's dad shook Eric's offered hand. "Come back anytime." He looked at Will and grinned. "With or without my son."

"Will do," Eric said after chuckling.

Will leant down and kissed his father's forehead. "See ya later, Dad."

"Drive safe," his dad said as they left via the garage door.

Eric climbed into Will's short-bed pickup and was in the process of buckling his seatbelt when Will climbed in. "I like them."

"Yeah, they're pretty great. I know I'm one of the lucky ones." Before putting on his seatbelt, Will leant over and kissed Eric. It didn't last as long as the one earlier in the evening, nor was it as intense, but it still made Will's cock take notice.

"Take me to somewhere where we can be alone," Eric whispered against Will's lips.

"I'm taking you home with me," Will answered. He gave Eric another soft kiss before pulling back. "I may not be able to take you out, but as long as we're careful, I see no reason why we can't spend time together."

"What about the case?"

Will buckled his seatbelt and put the sedan in reverse. He hated to confess to Eric how frustrated he was with the case. Other than his suspicion that Fallon and Jigger knew each other before moving to town, he'd pretty much come up empty. Short of another victim or an eyewitness coming out of the woodwork, he knew he didn't have enough to convince Byron to retry Jigger. What he did know was that he felt something special towards Eric, and that more than anything should prove to anyone who found out just how hard he'd worked to find evidence.

Driving towards his side of town, Will continued to war with himself. Eric deserved to know the truth. If not coming up with enough evidence to convict Jigger was going to come between them, it was better to find out sooner rather than later. "I haven't found anything concrete to go to Byron with," he admitted. "After the hung jury, my dad told me that I needed to paint a picture of Jigger for the jury. That I needed to prove to them that Jigger was as evil as we believe him to be." He shook his head. All detectives wanted to believe that the good guy came out on top and they would always find the evidence to take down the bad guys, but it wasn't always the case.

"You're telling me that he's not going to be tried again, aren't you?" Eric asked, the question sounding more like a statement.

"I'm sorry. I know I've let you down, but I didn't find a single person in Loveland who had anything bad to say about Jigger. Even the policeman who originally arrested him for stealing that car said he felt bad that Jigger had taken the rap for those older boys."

"What about the connection between Fallon and Jigger? Maybe I wasn't Jigger's first. If anyone knows, it's probably Fallon."

"Fallon testified that he didn't know about Jigger's use of Rohypnol at the bar. If he goes back on that now, he could be charged with perjury, and I can promise that Fallon knows that."

"You can't just drop it, Will. I can't stand the thought of Jigger getting away with what he did to me."

"I don't plan to drop it until I'm ordered to, but I'm afraid the time's coming, and I wanted you to be prepared if it does."

Chapter Five

After parking behind the house in front of the detached garage, Will led Eric in through the back door. Eric was still stunned at the idea that Jigger could very well get away with what he'd done to him and Becket.

Will cleared his throat, and Eric realised he was still standing in the doorway. "You're disappointed in me, aren't you?" Will asked.

Eric took a few steps into the warmth of Will's home and shut the door. "It's not you I'm disappointed in. I guess it's the system. I mean, I know why things are the way they are but it doesn't make it okay."

"I'll ask my captain if I can interrogate Fallon. Who knows, maybe we'll get lucky and he'll hand us all Jigger's dirty laundry in one basket."

Eric didn't know Fallon well, but he doubted the man would crack under pressure. "Fallon seems a little too cool to implicate himself in a lie."

"We won't know until I try." Will opened the fridge and removed two bottles of beer. He headed out of the kitchen and nodded at the doorway. "Let's go into the living room."

"Are you holding that beer hostage?"

Will paused and waved the beer at Eric in a teasing manner. "Come with me or you'll never see this again."

"You goof, I'd go with you even if you didn't have a beer." He walked over and snatched the bottle out of Will's hand. "But I'd prefer to have both of you."

Will took a moment to close the blinds and curtains before joining Eric on the sofa. "What do you usually watch?" he asked, turning on the television.

"I don't have a TV in my room, so I'm used to watching whatever the guys have on downstairs." Eric took a gulp of his beer. "Why's it okay for me to drink with you but not in my room?"

Will scooted closer, took Eric's beer out of his hand, and set it on the table. He sat back and wrapped his arms around Eric. "Because drinking makes you horny, and unless you're with me, I worry."

Deciding to go for it, Eric channelled his inner porn star and climbed on Will's lap. He draped his arms over Will's shoulders and leaned in. "I've spent the majority of this past week so drunk I passed out before ten o'clock and not once did I leave the house in search of someone else."

Will groaned and closed the distance, bestowing a hot, open-mouthed kiss on Eric. Mmm. Eric loved the taste of beer on Will's tongue and sucked it into his mouth. The move obviously surprised Will, who stiffened before giving in to Eric's passion.

Eric felt Will's erection pressing against him and longed to explore and taste it before something else happened and Will pushed him away again. He broke the kiss and began sliding off Will's lap, his hand on Will's zipper. "Will you let me touch you?"

With Eric kneeling on the floor in front of him, Will stood and toed off his sneakers before unzipping his jeans and pushing them—along with his underwear—down and off.

Eric's breath caught in his throat as he stared at the gorgeous cock. "Oh. My. God."

With a soft chuckle, Will sat down and spread his legs, making room for Eric to move in between them. "You're free to explore all you want, but don't feel you have to do anything that makes you uncomfortable."

It was Eric's turn to laugh. "You have absolutely no idea how many streaming porn videos I've watched since you kissed me." He drew his finger slowly down the length of Will's cock from tip to base. "You're a lot bigger than I am."

"But I'm sure not as big as some of those guys in the videos you've been watching."

Eric cupped Will's sac and marvelled at its weight. "Some of those cocks are gross and no way would I want them inside me." He leant forward and touched his tongue to the rivulet of pre-cum that ran down the head. The taste exploded in his mouth, proving to himself, once again, that despite his years of hiding, he was indeed gay.

A soft groan from Will filled Eric with confidence, prompting him to capture the crown in his mouth. The skin was soft and warm against his tongue as more pre-cum coated his throat. The videos he'd watched over and over came to mind, and Eric slid his lips as far down Will's length as he could manage. He stayed there for a few seconds before pulling back. Will's cock slipped from his mouth, showing Eric's inexperience. Embarrassed, he looked up into Will's eyes.

Will's response couldn't have been more perfect. He brushed Eric's cheek with his thumb while guiding his dick back to his mouth. The kindness and raw need in his expression said more than his words ever could. "You're doing great."

Pleased with himself, Eric tried once again to emulate the porn stars he'd watched do it with ease.

Will reached for Eric's hand and wrapped it around the base of his erection. "It'll give you more control," Will instructed.

Eric nodded and squeezed the blood-filled cock. It only took a few moments for him to establish a rhythm and depth he was comfortable maintaining.

"Eric," Will gasped. "I need...you gotta..." He gripped the back of Eric's head, burying his fingers in Eric's hair and pulled.

Eric shook his head, refusing to do the work without receiving the reward. Instead of withdrawing his mouth from Will's cock, Eric increased his suction.

With a loud groan and shout of, "Jesus," Eric's mouth was suddenly filled with the slightly bitter taste of Will's cum. His own body shook as a feeling of euphoria spread through him. It took a moment for the feeling to pass and once it had, he realised he'd just come in his jeans. *Fuck!*

Eric swallowed as fast as he could, but wasn't practiced enough to do it neatly. Before he gagged and made a total ass of himself, he pulled back and wiped his chin. It wasn't until he started to slide up to sit beside Will that he remembered he'd cum in his pants. He crossed his hands over the front of his jeans and tried to hide his embarrassment.

With his eyes still closed, Will reached for him, but Eric shrank back. "I can't," Eric said.

Will sat up and stared at Eric. "What's wrong?"

The concern in Will's voice made Eric feel like an idiot. He hadn't meant to alarm Will. It was obvious Will was worried that he'd pushed Eric into doing something he hadn't been ready for, but nothing could've been farther from the truth. He glanced down at his lap. "I made a mess of myself."

Will reached down and nudged Eric's hands out of the way. "That's not something to be ashamed of. It's a turn-on to know you were so into the pleasure you were giving me that you came."

Eric moved up to sit beside Will on the couch, and Will immediately wrapped him in his arms, taking his mouth in a deep kiss. He shared the taste of cum with Will, knowing he'd never forget the moment. Breaking for air, he grinned. "That was way better than watching porn."

Will chuckled. "Any day of the week," he agreed.

* * * *

Will pulled Eric's clothes out of the washer and tossed them into the dryer while Eric watched another episode of *Teen Wolf*. "About another forty-five minutes or so," he announced, walking back into the living room.

Clad only in a blanket, Eric nodded. "Thanks."

Will settled beside Eric and pulled him into his arms. He knew Eric was still embarrassed by what had happened, so they hadn't mentioned it again and had instead started a marathon of *Teen Wolf*. Eric had made fun of Will for watching the show until he'd finished the first episode. Will knew the weekly remake was probably meant for younger audiences, but he loved the damn thing and from the look of it, so did Eric.

Eric snuggled against Will's side and tilted his chin up for a kiss. Since the blowjob, they had indulged in a lot of kissing, but Will had tried his best to keep his hands to himself. After everything Eric had been through and the realisation that he was still so incredibly new to sex, the last thing Will wanted was to push him into something he wasn't ready for. As their kiss intensified, Eric moved to straddle Will's lap, losing his blanket in the process.

Will ran his hands down Eric's bare back, stopping just short of his ass. He broke the kiss and stared into Eric's eyes. "You're killing me."

Eric shook his head and began to move his hips, grinding himself against Will. "Touch me."

Will had read the hospital report dozens of times, so he knew what kind of injuries Eric had suffered at Jigger's hands. Although he had no doubt Eric's physical wounds had healed in the months since the rape, he couldn't stop worrying about the psychological damage.

Will slid his hands further down Eric's back to land on his ass. He cupped Eric's butt and waited for any sign of distress.

"I don't remember it," Eric whispered, unbuttoning Will's shirt. "It's not the fucking that bothers me; it's the fact that I didn't have a choice." He pushed Will's shirt off his shoulders. "This, with you, is what I want."

Will shrugged the rest of the way out of his shirt and dropped it to the floor. "Then let's go into the bedroom," he conceded.

After another deep kiss, Eric climbed off Will's lap. He started to reach for the blanket to cover himself, but Will stopped him with a hand on his forearm.

"Wait," Will said, getting his first real look at Eric's body. "Goddamn, you're sexy." He scooted to the edge of the sofa and slid his hands down Eric's lean, smooth chest to settle on his hips. Leaning in, Will kissed a path down Eric's stomach to his groin. He ran his tongue up Eric's length before taking the tip of Eric's cock into his mouth.

"Please don't make me embarrass myself again."

After another swipe of his tongue against the spongy head, Will released Eric's cock and gazed up at him. "There's something you need to learn," he began, getting to his feet.

Eric snorted. "There're a lot of things I need to learn."

Will clasped Eric's hand and led him towards the bedroom. He waited until he'd undressed and climbed into bed with Eric to continue. On his side, with Eric lying on his back, Will pushed the sheet off Eric's body. "Never be afraid of embarrassing yourself. If you don't feel comfortable enough with a lover to do or ask for what you want, chances are, you shouldn't be in bed with them in the first place."

Eric rolled to his side and buried his face against Will's neck. "It's easy for you to say something like that. You've been with other guys, so you know what the hell you're doing."

Will pulled Eric closer and insinuated his leg between Eric's thighs. "You did a pretty damn good job of blowing me. Sex is natural. Just listen to your body and follow your instincts."

When Eric didn't comment, Will decided to test the waters. He still wasn't sure how much Eric could comfortably handle, so he decided to go slow. Moving his hand in a circular motion, Will rubbed the muscled cheeks of Eric's ass.

Automatically, Eric hitched his leg higher on Will's hip, making it easier for Will to trail his fingers up and down the crack. Each time Will's fingers brushed across his hole, Eric's body shuddered slightly. "That feel good?"

Eric nodded, still hiding his face. It was obvious to Will that despite his words, Eric was still battling embarrassment. Instead of trying to talk to Eric again, Will rolled to his back and reached for the small lamp on the bedside table. He switched off the light, sending the room into darkness. "Better?"

"Yeah," Eric admitted.

Will reached into the drawer and removed a half-empty bottle of lube. "Do you trust me?"

"Of course."

Will didn't intend to fuck Eric, at least not yet, and wondered if it would help Eric settle if he knew. "Roll over and stick your ass in the air for me. I just want to touch and taste you. There'll be plenty of time later to ease into anything more."

"It's okay if you want to make love to me," Eric said, doing as Will asked.

Will's finger rubbed against Eric's hole, feeling the scar tissue left behind by his brutal rapist. "I'm making love to you right now. Fucking is one way to do that but not the only way."

Although Eric didn't say anything, he let out a soft moan.

Separating the cheeks of Eric's ass, Will ran the flat of his tongue against the scarred hole, wondering if the recently healed wounds still caused Eric pain. "I have to ask you something, and I need you to be honest."

"Okay," Eric agreed.

"Does it hurt when you go to the bathroom?" Will asked between licks, trying to keep Eric calm.

It took several moments for Eric to answer. "Sometimes, but not always."

Will swirled his tongue around the puckered skin before reaching for the bottle of lube. He applied more than he'd normally use to his fingers and closed the cap. "Touch yourself for me," he said, hoping to make the experience as pleasurable as possible for Eric.

"If I touch my dick I'll come," Eric said.

"That's okay. Coming is the payoff." Will eased the tip of his finger into Eric's hole. "Just let me know if you feel any pain."

Will continued to massage the outer ring of muscles using a gentle touch until his finger was inside to the second knuckle. "Okay?"

"Mmm-hmm," Eric moaned.

After several minutes of easing his finger in and out, Will's cock was as hard as a rock. "Here, let's try something else."

Will removed his finger and slapped Eric's ass playfully. "Climb over me and suck my cock."

Eric released the hold he had on his own cock and moved to allow Will to stretch out on the bed. "Sixty-nine?" he asked with excitement in his voice.

"Only if you want to." Will reached for the lube while Eric repositioned himself. He applied more slick to his fingers before guiding Eric's cock to his mouth. Groaning at his first real taste of Eric's pre-cum, Will reached between Eric's legs and found his partially stretched hole.

Eric engulfed Will's cock like he'd been sucking dick his entire life. Will groaned again as he slowly added another finger to Eric's ass. He swallowed Eric's cock to the root before pulling back for a breath. "I'm not going to last long," he warned.

Despite the blowjob Eric had given him earlier in the evening, Will's cock was ready to explode. He found Eric's prostate and rubbed the sensitive gland.

Eric's entire body bucked, shoving his cock further down Will's throat, he came without warning. No stranger to a mouthful of cum, Will skilfully allowed the thick strands to shoot down his throat without gagging.

Somewhere in the process of swallowing every drop of seed Eric had to offer, Will's own climax overtook him. He shook with the intensity of his orgasm as he pulled Eric's cock from his mouth and tried to catch his breath. "Fuck," he said, gasping for air.

Eric cleaned Will's cock with his tongue before turning around to drop down on Will's chest. The two of them said nothing for several minutes before Eric finally spoke. "Was that better?"

Will rubbed Eric's back. "If it had been any better, my head would've blown off."

"Which head?" Eric asked, chuckling.

"Both."

* * * *

After falling into an exhausted sleep, Eric was the first to wake. He lay against Will's chest and grinned like a fool. It had been the best night of his entire life, and although he wasn't ready for it to end, he needed to get back to BK House. It had been a busy weekend and he suddenly realised he hadn't finished his homework. *Shit!* Rusty had been right, he should've taken care of it on Friday night before he started drinking. Eric had stupidly assumed he'd have plenty of time before his Monday class.

Trying to ease out of bed without waking Will, Eric banged his knee on the corner of the side table. "Shit!"

Will bolted upright and turned on the light. "What's wrong?"

Shaking his head, Eric rubbed his injury. "Nothing, sorry. Your table just attacked my knee. I'm fine."

"Where're you going?" Will asked.

"Home. If I leave now, I'll make it before the sun comes up." Eric stood and started towards the door.

"Not so fast," Will sprang out of bed and stopped Eric before he could leave the room. "If you want to stay, you're more than welcome to."

"Thanks, but I have a couple things to do before class." He clasped his hands behind Will's neck and pulled his head down for a kiss. Although it had been several hours since he'd come in Will's mouth, he could still taste traces of his seed on Will's tongue. His body started to respond and before he knew it, his cock was hard and ready for another round. Unfortunately, he had other things to do.

Breaking the kiss, Eric reluctantly pulled back. "You're so damn tempting, but I really need to go."

With a loud sigh, Will nodded and reached for his jeans. "Go get dressed and I'll put on some shoes."

"I can walk. It's really not that far."

"Bullshit. After what happened on campus, there's no way you're walking alone."

Eric nodded his acceptance. "I'll meet you in the kitchen."

While Will dressed, Eric found his clothes and put them on. He found several other shirts and jeans in the dryer and took the time to fold them, feeling blissfully domestic.

"You didn't have to do that," Will said from the doorway.

Eric shrugged. "I didn't mind." He went to stand in front of the man he'd do anything for. "Ready?"

"Not really. I like having you here." Will rested his hands casually on Eric's hips, his expression turning serious. "As soon as I find the evidence to put Jigger behind bars, I'd like to see how far things can go between us. Are you comfortable with that?"

It suddenly hit him. He'd barely thought of Jigger all evening. For the first time since the rape, he felt like he could actually move on with his life. Although he still wanted Jigger to pay for what he'd done, Eric knew he didn't want a relationship with Will to be contingent upon whether or not Will found enough evidence to retry Jigger.

"Promise me something?"

Will's brow furrowed. "Okay."

"If you don't find anything new in the next week or so, tell Byron Long he should drop the case," Eric pleaded.

"Why would you want that?"

"Because Jigger's already stolen a piece of my life that I'll never be able to get back. I think I'm ready to move forward, and I can't—*we* can't," he corrected, "do that until this investigation is over."

"I've let you down, haven't I?" Will asked.

"No, just the opposite, actually. You've given me a reason to put the past behind me. I'm not naïve. I know rapists get away with this shit all the time, and millions of people learn to get on with their lives, knowing the truth but unable to do anything about it."

"I won't let you down," Will said.

"That's just it, you haven't. You've done so much more for me than any other detective would. Hell, you flew to Colorado for me. How many cops would do something like that?" Before Will could answer, Eric continued. "All I'm saying is that if you don't find anything else, I can live with it as long as I don't lose you because of it."

Will shook his head. "You won't lose me no matter what, but until I'm ordered to stop looking by Byron or my captain, I don't plan to give up."

* * * *

Eric spent the rest of the day thinking about what Will had said. Although he wasn't surprised by Will's answer, he knew there had to be another way. After a short phone call with Will, Eric was more determined than ever.

It seemed Fallon refused to speak to Will, and Will's captain refused to give Will the authority to drag Fallon into the station for formal questioning. Eric decided it was time to be proactive in the investigation.

Dressed in his sexiest clothes — which wasn't saying much, but they were the best he had — Eric left the house and took a cab to Fallon's on Fifth. It was barely nine o'clock, so the place was still rather empty when he walked into the swanky club.

Eric spotted Fallon immediately, but didn't want to pounce on him with questions, knowing Fallon would only clam up if he felt pressured. Finding a small table just off to the left of Fallon's position at the bar, Eric ordered a beer from the passing waiter.

Purposely turning his attention away from Fallon, Eric spotted Professors Ryan and Corto Delgado. He almost went over to say hi, but realised it would throw off his plan. There wasn't any doubt in his mind that Fallon would eventually approach him, the only question was when. He received his beer and reached for his wallet, but the waiter told him it was on the house, compliments of the owner.

It was Eric's cue. He turned towards Fallon and lifted his glass in thanks before taking a swig. He returned his attention to the professors. It appeared they were locked in a serious discussion, but he couldn't hear anything of what was being said.

"Are you waiting for someone?" a strong voice said from behind Eric.

Eric peered over his shoulder to find Fallon. "No, just needed to get out of the house."

Fallon gestured to the chair beside Eric. "May I?"

"Sure, I guess." Eric sat up straighter and took another drink.

"I had a visit today from your friend, Detective James."

Eric tried to act surprised. "I had no idea, and I wouldn't call him a friend." He tried to keep his voice neutral as he lied. He'd never been good at it, so he hoped Fallon bought it.

Fallon scooted his chair closer to Eric's. "I really am sorry about what happened to you. If it helps, my business hasn't really been the same since the news hit the papers."

It didn't, but Eric continued to keep his cool. "I'm sorry to hear that. It really is a beautiful place."

"So why don't you tell me why you're really here?" Fallon asked with suspicion.

Shit. Eric knew he was a second away from being busted. *Think fast*, he told himself. "I've been going to therapy, and my shrink told me I needed to really face what happened. I thought coming here would help jog my memory."

Fallon's light brown eyebrows lifted slightly. "And has it?"

Eric shook his head. "The only thing I remember from that night is sitting at that bar over there and seeing Jigger's face as he put me into the backseat of his car."

"You remembered Jigger? Why didn't that come out during the trial?"

"Because I didn't remember it until afterwards." He shrugged. "Still not enough to retry him, so it doesn't do me much good." Deciding to make his move, Eric leaned towards Fallon. "Can I ask you something?"

"Yes."

"Do you remember seeing me that night? Did I pass out at the bar or did I leave?"

Fallon shook his head. "I've already told Detective James everything I remember. You were there drinking and the next time I looked around you were gone. I didn't think a thing about it until the cops showed up looking for Jigger."

Eric took a deep breath and decided to push harder. "Did anyone ever accuse Jigger of raping them when you knew each other back in Louisiana?"

"Not that I..." Fallon's eyes narrowed as he stared daggers at Eric. "How do you know we knew each other in Louisiana?" He reached over and grabbed Eric's wrist, squeezing it in a bruising grip. "You lied to me. You are here poking around for the detective."

Eric tried to pull away from Fallon's hold. "I'm trying to find the truth about what happened that night. I don't think Becket was Jigger's first victim, and I can't believe you would think so either."

Fallon squeezed Eric's wrist tighter, causing Eric to cry out in pain. "Get out of my club and don't ever come back."

A shadow fell over the table and the next thing Eric knew, Manuel had Fallon's neck in his big hands. "Release him."

Fallon did as instructed and Adam quickly pulled Eric away from the table. Manuel bent down and spoke into Fallon's ear. "If you ever touch him again I'll snap your fucking neck."

"Get out," Fallon croaked.

Manuel released Fallon and took a step towards Eric and Adam. "You okay?"

Eric rubbed his bruised wrist. "Nothing broken, but I'd appreciate it if you could give me a ride."

Manuel nodded. "Absolutely." He pulled his wallet out of his pocket and tossed several bills at Fallon. "Here's the money for our drinks. Don't worry, we'll never be back."

Adam and Manuel led Eric out of the club. The moment they rounded the corner to the parking lot, Eric started to tremble.

"Are you sure you're okay?" Adam asked, lifting Eric's arm to study the blossoming bruise in the security light mounted on the building.

Eric started to tell them he was just shaken when he spotted a car in the back of the lot. A rush of fear enveloped him as he recognised the vehicle from his dream. Pulling away he started in the opposite direction, needing to get as far away as his unsteady legs would carry him.

"Stop," Manuel said, wrapping an arm around Eric's waist and easily lifting him off the ground. "You're safe now."

Eric shook his head and pointed towards the sedan. "Jigger's here."

Manuel and Adam turned their attention to the car. "You sure?"

Eric nodded. "I need to get out of here."

Eric tried to wiggle out of Manuel's embrace, but the big Spaniard wasn't having it. Instead, Manuel bent and scooped Eric into his arms and headed for his Lexus. "Open the door," he instructed Adam.

"Should I call the police?" Adam asked.

Despite his need for Will, Eric knew he couldn't ask the professors to drop him at Will's house. "Just take me home."

When Manuel lifted him into the backseat, Eric had another flashback of the night he was raped. Memories of Jigger arguing with Fallon while he lay naked and bleeding on the floor of a storage room assaulted him. Eric cried out, remembering how he'd clung to Jigger while being carried to the car.

"No!" Eric screamed.

* * * *

Will screeched to a halt in front of BK House and jumped out. He bounded up the steps and into the house without knocking. "Where is he?"

Jack, who was sitting in the living room with Charlie and two men Will didn't know, got to his feet and rushed over. "He's upstairs with Becket and Locky, but he hasn't spoken a word since Manuel and Adam brought him home."

Will recognised Adam's name as the one who'd called him and told him about the altercation with Fallon. He didn't take the time to shake hands with either man, more concerned for Eric. "Which room?"

"Two-oh-six," Charlie said.

Taking the steps two at a time, Will was outside Eric's closed door in seconds. He knocked before opening it. Eric was curled up on the bed with Becket's arms around him and Locky sitting at the foot of the bed.

"Hey, babe," Will said, moving to kneel on the floor beside the bed. He brushed Eric's hair away from his face. "Are you okay?"

Eric glanced from Will to Locky. "I need to talk to you alone," he said in a voice so soft Will barely heard him.

Will turned to Locky. "Can I have a minute with him?"

Locky stood and held out his hand to Becket. "We'll be downstairs if you need us."

Before leaving the room, Becket wiped tears from his eyes and leant over to kiss Eric's forehead. "It'll be okay. Will won't let anything happen to you."

"Thanks," Eric said without looking away from Will.

The moment Becket and Locky were out of the room, Will kicked off his shoes and climbed in bed behind Eric. He spooned around his lover and wrapped him in a protective embrace. "Adam told me about the argument with Fallon."

Eric shook his head and turned over to face Will. "Fallon was there that night."

"When Jigger raped you?" Will pulled Eric closer.

"Yeah," Eric said after a few moments. "But I don't think he was the one who hurt me. I think that was Fallon."

Will had a feeling Eric was transferring his earlier trauma at Fallon's hands to the night he was raped. "Honey, it was Jigger's cum that they found on your jeans, not Fallon's."

Eric shook his head. "No, I'm not saying Jigger didn't fuck me. Hell, for all I know the entire bar had a go at my ass. I just know in my heart that Jigger wasn't the one who hurt me."

Will took a deep breath. Having been intimate with Eric, the details of the rape were even harder to listen to, but the detective in him needed to know everything. "Tell me exactly what you remember."

Eric closed his eyes. "I remember the sound of a slamming door waking me up. I was on the floor in a room with stacks of boxes. I think they must've been liquor bottles, because Fallon was holding one in his hand. It was covered with blood, but I couldn't figure out where it had come from until Jigger grabbed it out of Fallon's hand and threw it against the wall. He screamed at Fallon, and told him he wouldn't take the fall for him if I died. The next thing I remember is Jigger picking me up and carrying me out the back door." Eric opened his eyes.

There was so much pain in Eric's gaze it nearly broke Will's heart. As much as he wanted to tell Eric everything would be okay, he couldn't bring himself to do it. He'd need a hell of a lot of proof before he could take the case to Byron Long. Fallon Bennett was from an incredibly wealthy and respected family, and there was no doubt he had enough well-paid lawyers to get him off.

"I'll need proof," Will finally said.

"I don't think you'll find any," Eric replied, sounding defeated.

"Then I'll have to get Jigger to turn against Fallon."

Chapter Six

After a trip to the emergency room to have Eric's wrist checked by a doctor and photographed for evidence, Will had taken him by the station to fill out an official complaint against Fallon.

"Now, as I told you before, I doubt anything will come from this, but at least it'll give me a reason to question Fallon," Will explained, handing the complaint over to Eric to sign.

Eric nodded. "Can I call Locky or Becket to pick me up before Fallon gets here?"

"Sure." Will turned his desk phone around and slid it towards Eric. He had a plan, but he'd need everything to fall smoothly into place for it to work.

Eric hung up. "They'll be here in a few minutes."

Despite Eric's willingness to go along with filing charges, Will still detected defeat in his voice. He rested his forearms on his desk and leant towards Eric. "I feel good about this."

"I hope so."

Will wished they were somewhere else. He longed to pull Eric into his arms and chase the shadows from his eyes. He stood and handed Eric his coat. "Come on, I'll walk you out."

Eric eased his bandaged wrist through the sleeve of his coat and winced. It was a reminder to Will of just how close Eric had come to getting seriously injured yet again. He wanted to yell at Eric for going to Fallon's club in the first place, but it wasn't the right time.

Before leaving his desk, he called dispatch and told them to pick up Fallon Barrett on a battery charge.

Stepping out of the police station, Will brushed his hand against Eric's. "I'll call as soon as I have something to tell you."

"Call even if you don't," Eric said, staring up at Will. "Okay."

Locky's car pulled in front of the station and Will led Eric to the car. He opened the door and spoke directly to Locky. "Just a sprain, but he's supposed to ice it."

"We'll take care of it," Locky assured him.

Sending Eric away was one of the hardest things he'd ever done, but he prayed it wasn't in vain. He shut Eric's door and placed his palm on the window before stepping back. There was still one more phone call to make, and he hoped his captain would go along with his plan.

* * * *

As he'd guessed, Fallon insisted on having his lawyer present before answering any of Will's questions. It gave Will the time he needed for Jigger to arrive with his own high-priced lawyer in tow.

"What's this about?" Jigger's lawyer, Chris Alton, asked.

Will had made sure the blinds had been left open in the interrogation room where Fallon sat waiting for his attorney. "I've discovered some new information and figured I'd talk to your client about it before contacting Byron Long in the morning."

Jigger's gaze went straight to Fallon. "What's he doing here?"

"That's what I wanted to talk to you about." Will showed Jigger into an adjoining interrogation room. "Have a seat," he told both men.

Will took his time fiddling with the video camera set up in the corner before moving to close the blinds between the rooms. He sat on the opposite side of the table, and pretended to look over a file.

"You didn't answer my question," Jigger finally said. "What's Fallon doing here?"

Will glanced up from his paperwork and grinned. "Singing."

"What's that supposed to mean?" Jigger shifted uncomfortably in the small metal chair.

"He has a lot to say about the night Eric Kloiber was raped."

"Bullshit," Jigger fired back.

Will shrugged. "We went over Fallon's on Fifth again and found traces of Eric's blood in the storeroom." He leant forward, staring at Jigger. "A room you both had keys to."

Of course it was a lie, but Jigger didn't need to know that. "Since he's the owner, we brought him in for questioning." Will shook his head. "Evidently, your ex-employer isn't the loyal friend you believe him to be."

"I don't know what he told you, and I'm not stupid enough to confess shit to you, but you should talk to Joshua Carlisle in Houma. Better yet, check out his hospital and bank records." Jigger stood and glanced at his lawyer. "Am I free to go?"

"Do you plan to level further charges against my client?" Chris asked.

"No, I'm not prepared to at this time, but I'm sure Byron Long will be in touch with you within a day or so." Will opened the door and watched Jigger and his lawyer walk out of the room. He turned back to Fallon and grinned. "Gotcha," he mouthed.

* * * *

Will was asleep outside Byron's office when a clearing throat woke him. He opened his eyes and stretched his arms over his head. "Morning."

Byron stared down at him. "Why do I feel like I'm walking into an ambush?"

"Beats me." Will got to his feet and tried to straighten his clothes. "I need a favour."

Byron unlocked the door to his office and ushered Will inside. "What kind of favour?"

"I need you to get me access to someone's medical records and bank accounts."

"Who?"

"Joshua Carlisle. He lives in Morgan City and worked as a volunteer at Barrett House for a while, which is owned and maintained by the Barrett family, as in Fallon Barrett."

"And?"

"Paul Williams told me to look up Joshua Carlisle when he believed Fallon was rolling over on him."

"Why would he think Fallon was talking to the police? Fallon hasn't helped us once during the entire investigation," Byron questioned, setting his briefcase down and taking a seat behind his desk.

Will grinned. "Oh, maybe because Fallon was sitting in one of the interrogation rooms last night when I called Paul's lawyer to bring him in for more questions."

Byron appeared totally confused. "I'm not following."

Will took a deep breath and took the time to explain the events of the previous night. Of course he left out the bits about kissing and holding Eric before they'd left for the hospital, but everything else was laid out on the table.

"Pretty smart," Byron said.

"I thought so. Now, can you get me access to Joshua Carlisle's information? I plan to call him, but I have a sneaky suspicion that he's not going to be very forthcoming with me."

"I'll see what I can do. I'm not going to lie, prosecuting Fallon Barrett won't be easy."

"I know, but if nothing else, it'll let him know we're onto him."

* * * *

Eric finished his last class and called Will. He'd spoken to him early that morning, but hadn't heard from him since.

"Hey," Will answered, sounding groggy.

"Did I wake you?"

"Yeah, I must've dozed off on the couch. How's your wrist?"

"Fine. Still a little swollen, but at least it's my left so I can still write and stuff." Eric glanced both ways before crossing the street. "So, did you find anything out about that guy Joshua?"

"Yeah, he's signed some sort of legal agreement that says he can't talk about Fallon, which tells me a lot. Byron's working on getting me a subpoena, so hopefully that'll come through tomorrow." Will yawned. "You on your way home?"

"Yeah, I'm almost there, but I'm sure I could be persuaded to stop by your house instead."

"I'd love it, but I think we should play it cool for the next few days, at least until I get access to Joshua's records, and I hand everything over to Byron."

Although Eric understood, he hated the thought of not seeing Will. "Do you really think that whatever Joshua's hiding will be convincing enough to convict him?"

"I don't know. Byron didn't seem to think so, but I'm holding out hope."

Eric sat on the front steps of BK House and shrugged out of his backpack. "If it's not enough, I'd rather just drop it, and move on."

"I know, and I'm not going to lie, it may come to that unless I can get a confession, which I doubt. It sounds like Fallon and Jigger have some sort of past, and even though Jigger gave me Joshua's name, I don't think he'd ever testify to anything in court."

Eric had already made peace with his anger over what had happened. The only reason he continued to push the case was because he knew the closure was important to Will. "You know, if Fallon gets away with it, there are other ways to punish him."

"I don't want to know," Will said.

Eric decided not to hatch 'Operation Destroy Fallon' until he had more proof, but he would definitely exact his revenge on the man who'd raped him once he knew for sure. "Can I call you later?"

"Why don't I call you before I go to bed, which will probably be in the next few hours?"

"Sounds good. Talk to you then." Eric hung up and put the phone in his pocket before picking up his backpack. He was getting ready to go inside when a taxi pulled up in front of the house.

"Hey," Rusty said, getting out of the cab. He waited for the driver to retrieve his luggage before climbing the steps.

"I thought you weren't coming back until the weekend?" Eric asked, taking one of Rusty's suitcases from him.

"My mom's sister, Virginia, showed up demanding my parents be buried properly, but I knew they didn't want that, so I called the funeral home and made arrangements to have their bodies cremated and their ashes shipped here." He grinned. "Then I told Virginia to shove her demands up her ass and to get the hell out of my house."

Eric's jaw dropped. "That doesn't sound like you at all."

"Right," Rusty giggled. "My mother hated her family because they disowned her when she married my dad. Heck, that was the first time I'd met the woman face to face. I couldn't believe she had the nerve to try and swoop in to get at their money. I told my dad's lawyer to pack up everything in the house and put it up for sale. I'll go through everything eventually, but I don't feel like dealing with the memories so soon."

Eric stared at Rusty. Despite his new friend's smile, Eric could tell there was a thick layer of sadness just below the surface. He opened the front door and waited for Rusty to get through the door before following him. "Does your aunt know you left?"

"Doubt it. Doesn't matter though because she doesn't know where I'm going to school. As far as I'm concerned, I'm on my own now."

"Not quite," Eric said, climbing the stairs towards their room. "You've still got me."

* * * *

After a quick shower to wash the stink of the day off him, Eric bounded down the steps for dinner. He walked into the dining room and stopped in his tracks. There were only five people at the table, Charlie, Jack, Becket, Locky and…Dane.

When Eric entered the room they all looked towards him, even Charlie. "What's going on?" Eric asked. It was the first time in months that Dane had visited the house, so he knew it wasn't a coincidence.

"Becket told me what my uncle did to you last night," Dane said.

Eric didn't want to have the conversation, not now, not with Dane. He held up his bandaged wrist. "I'm fine, it's just a sprain."

"It's more than that, and I think everyone at this table knows it," Locky replied.

Eric shook his head. "I'm not talking to you guys about this." He turned and bolted from the room. He barely made it to the front sidewalk when the door opened and Becket and Dane came spilling out of the house.

"If you're hiding something, don't you think I have a right to know?" Becket called after him.

Shit! Eric turned to face Becket and Dane. "I remembered things last night when Manuel helped me into his car."

Dane shoved his hands in his front pockets. "About the night you were raped?"

Eric nodded. "I can't talk to you about it. I'm sorry, I don't mean to sound like an asshole, but I just can't."

Dane's eyes filled with tears. "It's about Fallon, isn't it?"

Eric swallowed around the lump in his throat. "I—I can't."

Becket glanced at Dane. "Give us a minute, will ya?"

Dane lifted his glasses and wiped at his eyes. "I'll be inside."

Becket pointed towards the porch swing. "Talk to me."

"Fallon fucked me with a wine bottle," Eric announced, sitting beside Becket.

Becket paled. "Are you sure?"

"No, I get off on making shit like that up. Of course, I'm sure. The problem is I can't prove it, no one can. Jigger was there, but I know for a fact it was Fallon who fucked me bloody."

Becket gripped the seat on either side of him and looked down at his feet. "The last thing I remember about that night is being in Fallon's apartment," he mumbled. "I guess when I didn't go to the police, he figured I didn't remember anything." He balled his hand into a fist and pounded it against his thigh. "Fuck!"

"He won't go to prison," Eric informed Becket, knowing in his heart that he was right. "My guess is neither will Jigger."

"So we're just going to let them get away with it?" Becket asked.

Eric glanced towards the house. "If I had it my way, I'd spray-paint 'Fallon's a Rapist' all over the fucking town, but Dane lives here, too."

"So what should we do?"

Eric stood and squared his shoulders. "I don't know about you, but I'm tired of being the victim. I say we march over to Fallon's and tell him exactly what we think of him."

"What'll that do? He knows we have no proof."

"Maybe not, but I want to look him in the eyes and tell him I know what he did to me." Eric put his hand to his chest. "I need that. I've earned it."

Becket got to his feet and pulled a set of keys out of his pocket. "Let's hope Locky doesn't mind us borrowing his car."

* * * *

Having fallen back to sleep after Eric's call, Will blindly reached for his ringing cell phone. He was so tired he couldn't get his eyes to focus on the display, so he answered it blindly. "James."

"Will, it's Locky. I think you should come over here."

"What's going on?" Will asked, reaching for his shoes.

"Eric and Becket just tore out of here in my car," Locky explained.

"Where're they going?" Will asked, grabbing his keys off the kitchen table on his way out the back door.

"Dane's here. Although Eric didn't come out and tell Dane his uncle had something to do with the rape, he refused to speak to Dane at all. Dane left Becket and Eric alone to talk and the next thing I know my tires are leaving rubber on the driveway."

Surely Eric wasn't reckless enough to confront Fallon in his own club. "I'm on my way. I'll swing by and pick you up."

* * * *

Becket pulled into the parking lot and turned off the ignition. "Let's do this."

Eric climbed out of the car and went to the front door of the club with Becket at his side. Fallon's on Fifth didn't open for another hour and a half, but that didn't stop Eric from pounding on the door with his fist.

When no one showed up to answer it, Eric switched to his foot, kicking at the artfully etched glass. "Open up, you sonofabitch!"

A shadow came from the back of the club and started towards the door. In no time, Fallon's smug face was looking at Becket and Eric through the glass. "Go away."

Eric shook his head. The rage that he'd kept suppressed for months came pouring out of him. "Not until I talk to you. Now open this goddamn door before I throw a fucking brick through it."

Fallon twisted the deadbolt and swung open the door. "You're just begging for me to call the police. I wonder who they'll believe this time."

"I don't give a flying fuck who you call," Eric said.

Fallon started towards the back of the room and slipped behind the bar. "Say your piece and get out."

As Eric and Becket watched, Fallon casually poured himself a glass of wine. Eric opened his mouth to say something, but Becket surprised him by grabbing the wine bottle and smashing it against the side of the bar.

Becket held the broken bottle with its jagged edges pointed towards Fallon's throat. "I hear you like to play with wine bottles."

Fallon's eyes went wide as he glanced back and forth between the bottle and Eric. "You remember?"

Eric's breath caught in his chest. It was a dangling thread he decided to pull until Fallon unravelled. "Yeah, and I know about Joshua Carlisle," he lied.

Fallon started to take a step back, but Becket, still holding the broken bottle, lunged towards him. "Don't you dare take another step."

"Josh signed a gag order and was paid handsomely for it, he'd never tell you or anyone else anything."

Eric moved around the bar to stand close enough to Fallon to stare him in the eyes without getting in the way of Becket and his makeshift weapon. "Why'd you do that to us?"

"I'm not saying anything else to either of you," Fallon stated, crossing his arms over his chest.

Eric would have to push and push hard. "Is your dick really that small that you have to drug someone and use a wine bottle to fuck them in order to get off? Is that the secret Josh knows about you? Did he catch a glimpse of your puny little cock and threaten to tell everyone?"

"Shut up," Fallon growled.

Eric knew he'd struck a nerve. He reached down and grabbed the front of Fallon's dress pants. Although Fallon's cock felt perfectly normal, Eric would never let him know it. "Shit, how do you even take a piss out of this little worm?"

Becket laughed and Eric continued. "No wonder you have the reputation of having a different guy every night. Who in the hell would come back to this little thing for seconds?"

"I should've let you bleed to death on the fucking floor!" Fallon screamed, spittle spraying as he ranted. Without warning, he pushed Eric towards the broken bottle.

As if in slow motion, Eric watched as his face neared the jagged edges. He turned his face to the side just as Becket pulled the bottle back, grazing his cheekbone with one sharp point. He heard Will scream his name, but everything happened too fast to answer. Although there wasn't immediate pain, he did feel the warmth of his blood as it ran down his face.

"Eric!" Will bellowed again, jumping over the bar to land beside Eric.

"Get Fallon," Eric said, cupping the side of his face. "Shoot the motherfucker if you have to."

"Call 9-1-1," Will shouted as he ran after Fallon.

Locky pulled his T-shirt over his head and pressed it against Eric's face before picking up the wall phone behind the bar.

Becket looked dazed, and Eric knew he was blaming himself for Eric's injury. "It wasn't your fault. Without you, there's no way he would've stood still long enough for me to get to him."

Locky hung up and took the bloody T-shirt out of Eric's hand. "Let me take a look."

"It doesn't hurt," Eric said, more for Becket's sake than Locky's. "Couple of stitches and I'll be fine."

"You think they'll arrest me?" Becket asked.

"No," Locky and Eric said at the same time.

"I think he needs you more than I do right now," Eric told Locky.

Locky nodded and moved around the bar to Becket's side. With Becket taken care of, Eric walked to the nearest table and sat down. He didn't move even when he heard the sirens stop outside the building. "It doesn't matter to me if they catch him or not."

"Huh?" Locky pulled his attention away from Becket long enough to ask.

"I know, and he knows I know, and that's enough for me."

"Well it's not enough for me," Will said, coming up from behind Eric. He pulled out a chair and sat down beside Eric. "He's in the back of a cruiser, and there are four people in this room who heard him say he should've left you to die that night." He reached under the table and squeezed Eric's thigh. "Let's get you to the emergency room."

"It was worth it," Eric said, letting Will help him to his feet.

"You scared ten years off my life," Will grumbled.

"Sorry about that, but it was still worth it."

* * * *

After another long night spent in the emergency room and at the police station, Will pulled to a stop behind his house. The sun wasn't up yet, but it was damn close. He struggled to get the driver's door open as exhaustion threatened to overtake him.

A movement on his small back porch caught his eye and he prepared himself for a fight. "Who's there?"

"Me," Eric said, sitting up. "I know I'm not supposed to be here, but I couldn't stay away."

Will pocketed his keys and his phone and went to help Eric to his feet. "How long have you been out here?"

Eric shrugged. "Couple hours. I fell asleep, so I'm not really sure."

With an arm wrapped around Eric's waist, Will dug his keys back out and unlocked the door. "So you know, there's a spare key under the rock in front of the shed."

"I'll remember that." Eric walked into Will's house and went straight to the bedroom.

Even though he knew he should take Eric home, Will couldn't bring himself to do anything but lock the door and follow him. He stopped by the bathroom and took a long piss before shrugging out of his clothes and joining Eric under the covers.

"Is Becket in trouble?" Eric mumbled, curling himself against Will.

"No." Will wrapped his arms around Eric. "Sleep first, talk later."

"Mmm-hmm," Eric agreed.

Will kissed the small bandage on Eric's cheek where he had received stitches to the small inch-sized cut and closed his eyes.

* * * *

"Will?" Eric called, walking into the bedroom.

Will opened his eyes. "Good morning," he mumbled.

Eric smiled and joined Will in bed. "It's afternoon and your captain's been calling for the last two hours."

Will's eyes sprang open and he sat up. "Shit. Why didn't you wake me?"

"I tried. Believe me, I tried. I even tried sucking your cock, but that didn't work."

"I don't believe you." He pushed back the covers and swung his legs over the side of the bed. "You didn't answer Vince's calls, did you?"

"No." Eric handed the phone to Will. "He left messages, too, but I didn't listen to them either."

Will glanced over his shoulder. "Sorry, I didn't mean to sound like I was jumping on you." He laid back and pulled Eric into a deep kiss. "Forgive me?"

"As long as I can get a few more of those," Eric answered.

"Definitely, but let me check my messages first."

Eric bided his time by writing dirty words with his finger on Will's broad back. He'd missed yet another day of classes, but he doubted he'd have any trouble making up the work. It was better than falling asleep during one of his lectures and being called out in front of a classroom full of people.

"They found traces of your blood in the storeroom," Will said over his shoulder.

"Makes sense seeing as that's where I almost bled to death," Eric quipped, instantly regretting it. "Sorry."

"You owe me a kiss."

"And I'll gladly pay that fine." Despite everything that had happened, or maybe because of it, Eric was in a fantastic mood. He felt lighter than he had in months and wasn't about to let thoughts of his rape, Jigger or Fallon drag him down.

"Shit," Will cussed and started hitting his numbered keypad.

"Something wrong?" Eric asked, pressing himself against Will's back.

"The information about Joshua came in, but Vince said he wasn't going to wait all day for me to answer the goddamn phone before opening it. I mean, it's bullshit, I already know Fallon raped the guy, but I needed the proof to give to Byron." Will barely took a breath before speaking again. "It's James. Sorry...yeah, but I haven't had much...I know, Vince

229

it wasn't intentional. Just tell me...why can't you...that's bullshit."

Eric waited anxiously for Will to get off the phone since he couldn't understand a darn thing they were talking about.

"Fine, whatever," Will barked into the phone before turning it off. He reared back as if to throw it against the wall but changed his mind and tossed it to the bedside table. He rolled to his side and swung his legs back up on the bed. "I'm off the case."

Eric bit his bottom lip. He hadn't been around surly Detective James for a while and wasn't sure how to approach him. "Is it because of me?"

"Yeah. Byron and Vince both suspect something's going on between us, and Byron doesn't want our relationship to, and I quote, 'muddy the water'."

"That's the same thing that little prick told Becket." Eric moved to lie beside Will. "Did he tell you anything else?"

"Because of the injuries Fallon inflicted on you, Byron wants him the most and is willing to make deals with Jigger to make it happen."

"So Jigger could go free after all?"

"I doubt it, but Byron could reduce the charges and prison term."

Eric remembered the concern in Jigger's eyes when he placed Eric in the car. "I'm satisfied with that, not that anyone cares."

"I care." Will hugged Eric against his chest.

Eric settled his head against Will and playfully petted the short hairs on his chest. "I know, but do you care enough to give me those kisses and the blowjob you owe me?"

"I'll agree to the kisses, but there's no proof you tried to give me a blowjob," Will teased.

Eric reached down and wrapped his hand around Will's hardening cock. "Fine, don't believe me, but I know the truth."

Will rolled them both until he was laying on top of Eric. "How about if I make it up to you?"

"That depends, are we talking about a blowjob or are you gonna finally fuck me?"

Will reached into the drawer beside the bed and removed a new box of condoms and the lube. "I've had these since I rescued your drunk butt from the park after Jigger's mistrial."

"Pretty sure of yourself, weren't you?" Eric teased, and pushed against Will's chest.

Will used his legs to spread Eric's before moving back to kneel between them. "Did I have a reason not be assured that you were hot for my body?"

Eric wasn't sure if it was lack of sleep or his near brush with the jagged edge of a bottle the previous night, but there seemed to be a lighter vibe in the room. "You know, when you came to the hospital to question me for the first time, I thought you were the grouchiest SOB, outside my dad, that I'd ever met."

"I probably was, I hadn't shagged a young college kid in a really long time." Will poured lube into his hand and began to prepare Eric's hole.

Eric moaned, forgetting all about their conversation. Taking care not to further injure his wrist, he hooked his forearms under his knees and lifted his legs against his chest. The way Will touched and teased his hole was incredibly intimate. Eric looked down the length of his body and watched Will closely. He'd been waiting for the right time to tell Will he was falling in love with him, but having a finger eased into his ass didn't seem to be it.

"Okay?" Will asked when he caught Eric staring at him.

"More lube," Eric instructed, proud of himself for asking. His scars weren't exactly painful, but they were still sensitive and at times tingly in an asleep sort of way.

With his free hand, Will opened the bottle and dripped more lube directly onto Eric's hole.

"Cold," Eric announced, jumping slightly.

"Don't worry, it'll warm up." Will started pushing lube into Eric's hole, making sure the scar tissue on the outside was heavily slicked as well.

When Will introduced another finger into Eric's ass, Eric couldn't help but ask. "How many of those do I have to take before I pass the test?"

Will glanced down at his cock. "Three, so just sit back and enjoy the ride."

It wasn't that Eric wasn't enjoying himself, far from it, but he'd dreamed for years of feeling a cock shoved inside him. The fact that Will would, at least in his mind, be his first, thrilled Eric to no end.

"Have you ever used a plug or a dildo?" Will asked.

Surprised at the out-of-the-blue question, Eric shook his head. "Where would I have stored it? I'd burst into flames if I'd tried to take something like that into my folks house, and I can only imagine what Ira would've done if he'd found a giant purple dildo in our dorm room."

Eric frowned, a thought occurring to him. "Are you saying I should get one?"

"Yeah, I am. Actually, I think it would help with your scars if you stretched them on a daily basis for a while."

"Oh, that's the kind of homework I wouldn't mind doing at all. Of course it would be a lot more fun if I had a sexy professor teach me how to do it right."

Will's answer was to pour more lube onto his fingers and gently ease a third in beside the first two. Oh, fuck, Eric's ass felt stuffed and Will was only in a couple of inches. What would it feel like to have all nine inches of Will's cock inside him? He shivered at the idea.

"Open one of those rubbers for me, would ya?" Will asked.

Eric reached beside him and picked up the box. "These are ribbed for her pleasure. Who's she and why does she get my pleasure?" Eric joked, fumbling with the foil wrapper. He turned the wrapper around and around, searching for a little slit like they had on the foil packets of fruit snacks. "How do you open this?"

"With your teeth usually." Will started to reach for the condom, but Eric pulled it back.

"I can do it." Eric used his teeth and eventually tore the damn thing open. He picked it up from his chest where it had jumped out of the package and looked at it closely. "These ribs don't look big enough to give anyone pleasure."

Will took the condom away from Eric and quickly rolled it down his length. "It's what's inside that really counts."

"You say that like an expert."

"No, just a man who's dying to fuck you." Will applied a generous amount of lube to the already-lubricated condom before placing the head of his cock at Eric's hole.

Before Will could issue the usual demand, Eric nodded. "I'll let you know if it's too much."

Will grinned. "You know me too well already."

Eric took a deep breath and slowly exhaled as Will's cock breached his outer ring of muscles.

"Push out," Will said between clenched teeth.

As Will's ginormous cock eased its way inside him, Eric suddenly had a whole new appreciation for women who gave birth. Not that it was the same hole or even travelling in the same direction, but it was amazing just the same. How his body managed to stretch to accommodate such a large cock was beyond Eric's realm of reasoning at the moment.

"Stop thinking so hard and relax."

Eric opened his eyes and looked up at Will. He didn't dare tell Will he was trying to keep his mind off the brief twinges of pain for fear Will would immediately pull out and never try again. "This is me relaxed. It doesn't get much more lax than this."

Halfway in, Will stopped and reapplied lube.

"Watch it or we're going to slide right out of bed," Eric warned.

Will chuckled. "Sorry, but your scars are starting to thin out a little too much. I'm afraid of reinjuring you."

"I'm fine."

"Yeah, that's what you said before. Indulge me." Will started moving in and out of Eric's ass with only four or five inches of his cock.

Although Eric wished he could take Will's entire length and girth, he trusted Will to do what he thought best. Will was right. The last thing Eric wanted was another trip to the hospital. No matter, Will definitely knew how to work his cock, the half that continued to fuck him deserved some sort of award.

Eric transferred one of his legs to Will's shoulder before reaching down to firmly grip his cock. "Try deeper," he begged. The last thing he wanted to be was the freak who couldn't take his man's entire length.

More cold lube was added to Eric's hole as Will continued to rock his way in a little more with each thrust. "That's it," Will gasped.

Eric wanted to scream with joy when he felt Will's sac slap against his ass for the first time. He was so excited he couldn't hold his climax at bay a moment longer. The first shot splashed onto his upper stomach followed quickly by several more. "Keep going," he urged, riding out his orgasm.

"Not for long," Will announced.

The look of pain on Will's face startled Eric. "Am I hurting you?"

Will shook his head. "Yeah, but it's a good pain."

Eric's ass burned like a motherfucker, so he had a good idea of what Will was talking about. He reached out and ran his fingertips down Will's chest to where they were joined. He wished he could see Will's cock sliding in and out of him. "You need a mirror on the ceiling," he said, glancing up.

"Fuck!" Will bellowed as he pushed deep into Eric's channel. He removed Eric's leg from his shoulder and collapsed on top of him, grunting with each burst of seed into the condom.

Eric, already recovered from his climax, buried his hands in Will's hair and whispered in his ear. "I love you."

Epilogue

Will was standing next to Eric as they waited for the courtroom to open for what they hoped would be the last day they'd ever have to see Fallon Barrett.

"Hey, son," Will's dad greeted, moving to stand next to him.

Will was impressed by his dad's attire. Rarely did he see his dad in anything but his uniform or an old pair of jeans, but Henry James was dressed in his finest Sunday clothes. "Someone die?"

His dad punched him in the arm. "I took the day off, so I could be here for Eric."

"You didn't need to do that, Mr James," Eric said.

"Yes, he did," Will disagreed. "It's probably the first vacation day he's taken off in the last ten years."

"You'd be wrong about that. I took your mom to Spokane three years ago for a long weekend."

"Oh, that's right, you actually took half a Friday off so you could beat some of the traffic," Will joked.

"Watch it."

Will bumped shoulders with his dad. "It's a nice thing to do, you old softy."

"Shut up," his dad growled before smiling.

Becket arrived with Locky and his brothers. Will recognised Cade from the car sitting outside his house the first night Eric had visited him. "What's he doing here?" he asked Eric.

Eric pinched Will's side. "Relax, he's here for Becket, not me."

"He'd better not be here for you." Will wasn't above jealousy and when Cade glanced at him before moving his gaze to Eric, his blood started to boil. The wink Cade shot Eric's way was going too far, and Will stepped in front of the larger-than-life cowboy. "You got a problem?"

"Nope," Cade said, the corners of his mouth lifting into a smile. "You?"

"Yeah, I guess I do."

Eric stepped between the two men. "Will, this is Becket's oldest brother, Cade. Cade, this is my extremely jealous but sexy as hell boyfriend, Will."

Eric's announcement took some of the fire out of Will, but he promised himself to keep an eye on Becket's oldest brother.

The doors opened and the crowd began to file in. Unlike Jigger's trial, Fallon's had been moved to a larger courtroom with a much bigger gallery. Although cameras weren't being allowed in the courtroom, there were several reporters and sketch artists. Thankfully, the judge issued them a warning against using Eric's name or likeness in the media.

"Come on, let's go," Eric urged Will towards the door.

They sat in the back of the courtroom each day they'd attended, which hadn't been every day. Eric had made it clear that he wouldn't miss any more classes because of Fallon or Jigger. It was an easy promise to keep in Jigger's case. His trial had lasted only two days on the lesser charge of assault. He'd been convicted and sentenced two months earlier.

Will knew Fallon Barrett's case was the crown jewel in Byron Long's career. And, although Will hated to admit it after being tossed from the case, Byron had done a damn fine job so far.

Eric sat beside Will and reached for his hand. The two of them had grown incredibly close over the last five months and planned to spend the summer together. Will had even put in for a two-week vacation so he could take Eric on a cruise.

The door opened and the jury filed in moments before the bailiff asked everyone to stand as the judge walked into the courtroom. Will squeezed Eric's hand, praying for the verdict they'd been hoping for.

"You may be seated," the judge said and turned his attention to the jury foreman. "Has the jury reached a decision?"

"We have, your honour." The foreman passed the bailiff a folded sheet of paper.

The bailiff approached the bench and handed Judge Westfall the verdict. After reading the paper and taking notes, the judge passed it back to the bailiff who gave it to the foreman once again.

Eric stood, leaned over, and whispered in Will's ear. "Remember, no matter what, we're out of here as soon as I finish finals."

Will nodded. "I'll remember."

* * * *

While everyone around him celebrated Fallon's guilty verdict, Eric sat in the game room, watching episodes of *Teen Wolf*. He'd asked Will for some time alone and so far, everyone had respected his request.

The one person he couldn't seem to get off his mind was Dane. Eric knew the trial had been hard for him and had wanted to call on more than one occasion, but Will said Byron Long would frown upon it. Now that he didn't have to worry about what the fuck Byron frowned upon, Eric reached for the phone and the student directory.

"Hello?" a deep voice answered, presumably Magnus.

"I'm sorry to bug you, but would you do me a favour and give Dane a message for me?"

"Who is this?" Magnus asked.

"Eric. Eric Kloiber. I just wanted to tell Dane I'm sorry."

"Just a minute."

Eric could hear Magnus' deep voice talking to someone in the background moments before Dane's voice came over the phone. "Eric?"

"Yeah. Look, I know it's a bad time, but I wanted you to know I'm sorry."

"You have nothing to be sorry for," Dane replied.

"I'm not sorry for what I've done, but I know how much you loved your uncle, and I'm sorry that this happened to your family," Eric tried to explain.

"Thank you. It takes a special person to think of their rapist's family on a day like this. I just want you to know, that even though what he did to you is unforgivable, he isn't all bad."

Eric didn't know what to say. "I guess I'll have to take your word on that. I just wanted you to know I was thinking of you."

Will walked into the room and gestured to the phone. "Who're you talking to?"

Having said everything he'd intended Eric held up his finger. "Okay, well, I guess I'll see you around then."

"Eric?" Dane said before Eric could hang up.

"Yeah?"

"I don't want things to be weird between us."

"Don't worry, they won't be." Eric smiled, knowing he hadn't lost his friend. He hung up and wiped his eyes.

"Dane?" Will asked.

Eric nodded. "I wanted to check in with him to see how he was doing."

"You ready to go back to my place?"

"Yep, but I need to throw some more clothes in a bag first. Before you know it, all my stuff'll be at your house."

"Is that such a bad thing?" Will followed Eric up the staircase.

"Don't start. I've already told you, I've got one more year of wild college life left and I plan to enjoy it." He entered his room and waved to Rusty who was lying on the bed with headphones on. The really strange thing about it was there was nothing at all plugged into the headphones, so basically, Rusty was listening to the sounds of his own blood rushing through his ears. *Odd.*

"But you don't do anything but hang at my house anyway," Will argued.

"Right, that's the wild college life I'm talking about. It wouldn't feel nearly as rebellious and naughty if I actually lived there." Eric threw a few T-shirts into his backpack before looking through his drawers. "I'm outta jeans, they must all be at your place. Remind me to do laundry when we get home."

"There, you said it."

"Said what?" Eric glanced at Rusty, wondering how much of their conversation his roommate could actually hear.

"Home, you called my house home."

"Did not." Eric grabbed an extra pair of sneakers so he could start jogging with Will in the mornings.

"Yes, you did." Will stopped in the middle of their discussion and pointed towards Rusty. "Can he hear us?"

"No, but he can sure as shit see you getting all red-faced," Eric pointed out.

"Maybe we should ask him if you said it," Will said, still staring at Rusty.

"You're crazy." Eric shouldered his backpack. "Ready?"

"I guess," Will said, shaking his head in frustration.

Eric winked at Rusty. "I'll call ya tomorrow."

"Okay, ya know the two of you have a strange relationship," Rusty muttered.

"I know, isn't it fun?" Eric practically skipped out of the room, happier than he'd ever been in his life.

About the Author

An avid reader for years, one day Carol Lynne decided to write her own brand of erotic romance. Carol juggles between being a full-time mother and a full-time writer. These days, you can usually find Carol either cleaning jelly out of the carpet or nestled in her favourite chair writing steamy love scenes.

Carol Lynne loves to hear from readers. You can find her contact information, website details and author profile page at http://www.total-e-bound.com.

Total-E-Bound Publishing

www.total-e-bound.com

Take a look at our exciting range of literagasmic™
erotic romance titles and discover pure quality
at Total-E-Bound.